STILL
BEATING

A LOST BOYS NOVELLA

JESSIE WALKER

Editing/Proofreading: Heather Caryn

Cover Design/Formatting: Jessie Walker

For those who wanted more.
This wouldn't exist if it weren't for you.

wail forever <3

PLAYLIST

"Los Angeles" - Midnight
"Believe In Dreams" - Flyleaf
"Lost" - Dermot Kennedy
"Under the Bridge" - Red Hot Chili Peppers
"Sunsetz" - Cigarettes After Sex
"Simple Man" - Lynyrd Skynyrd
"Daylight" - Shinedown
"Are You Lonesome Tonight?" - Elvis Presley
"Dirt" - Alice In Chains

And more...

Check out the full playlist on Spotify

AUTHOR'S NOTE

Please note that this is <u>not</u> a standalone. This novella picks up almost immediately where the Epilogue in *If There's A Way* left off, with the Lost Boys out in Los Angeles, recording their first album. If you've yet to read the duet, it's highly, highly recommended you stop here.

This isn't an extended epilogue. Not everything will be wrapped up nicely. This is part of a true series that is heavily character-driven and takes place in "real-time."

Will and Way might be more solid than ever, as individuals and as a couple, but they're still growing. They're still healing.

Their lives have really only just begun.

Triggers for this novella can be found at the back of his book, following the Acknowledgments, or on the author's website.

www.authorjessiewalker.com

⚡

Lost Boys Series Recommended Reading Order:

Where There's A Will
If There's A Way
Still Beating
Every Breath After — coming soon!

"Rhythm is sound in motion.
It is related to the pulse, the heartbeat, the way we breathe.
It rises and falls.
It takes us into ourselves; it takes us out of ourselves."

—Edward Hirtsch

1

WILL FOSTER

IT'S THREE A.M. WHEN I get the call.

I wish I could say it woke me from a dead sleep, but I'm lucky if I get more than a couple hours of undisturbed shut-eye these days.

"Sorry to wake you," the familiar voice says down the line, his tone hushed and unsure.

I rub an eye, pushing up on my arm as I strain to hear him. Wherever they are, it's loud. It's not helping that he seems to be whispering.

"S'fine. What's wrong? Is he okay?" My voice cracks, and I wish I could say it's from sleep.

Mason blows out a breath. "Yeah, he's... he's fine. He just—"

"Then what?" I cut in roughly, sitting up straighter, fully awake now. "What happened?"

On a good day, I need at least two cups of coffee before my patience kicks in.

On a bad day...

I pinch the bridge of my nose, trying to rein in my frustration.

But can't he just fucking spit it out already?

As soon as I saw the name flashing across my screen, I knew something happened. Mason doesn't just call me to chat about nothing, especially knowing how late it is for me here.

He doesn't say anything right away, and I'm just about to really lose my cool on him when he finally blurts, "He's having a panic attack." A beat passes. "I think."

Everything in me grinds to a halt. "Where is he?"

"Right here. Next to me. We're at a diner. Everything was going okay, and then someone dropped a frying pan, I think,

STILL BEATING (PAPERBACK)

in the kitchen." He huffs, and it's only now I can make out the frustration in his voice. "It was loud and sudden and—"

"Like a gunshot," I finish softly as images rush to the forefront of my mind. Memories I'd do anything to purge the fuck out from both our heads, Waylon's and mine.

"Yeah."

Loud sudden noises don't always get to him, but when they do...

I don't even realize I'm jumping out of bed, flipping on the lights, and rushing over to my dresser.

Our dresser.

I've been living in the apartment above O'Leary's for several weeks now. Just under a month. But it's only been ten days since I've had the place all to myself.

I fucking hate it.

The silence...

It's deafening.

Terrifying.

The electric bill is going to be sky-high after this month, what with me leaving the television and random lights on at all hours of the day. Just to give me some sense of comfort.

My hands are grabbing things without me even really registering what they are. I tuck the phone between my ear and shoulder as I tug on a pair of black sweats, not even checking to see if they're mine, let alone right side on. "Put him on."

"He's not—"

"Just hold it up to his ear."

A beat passes, then I hear a shuffle through the phone. I run my hand through my hair, blinking rapidly against my own rising panic as I wait.

And wait some more.

I hear muffled voices. Mason's. Shawn's.

But not Waylon's.

Fuck.

I've never been so acutely aware of just how fucking far away from me he is until this moment, and time is moving at a fucking snail's pace. Slowing down with each dragging second I don't have him in my arms. Every beat of my heart that I don't hear his voice, see his dimples, feel his warm body against mine.

Sure, I've missed him like crazy in the last week and a half he's been in LA. Counting down the days until I could see him again.

Just nine more days.

Just six more days.

And now...

Three more fucking days.

But this is different. This is every fear and worry I've had since I dropped him off at the gate, sling-shotting to the front of my brain. Blotting out any rational thought.

STILL BEATING (PAPERBACK)

How will I ever make it to Saturday after this?

Sure, we knew this could happen. Hell, it wasn't so much an *if*, but a *when*. One we planned for as best we could.

And now it's time to put our plans to the test.

A noise reaches my ears, like a frustrated growl, or groan, coming deep from within his chest, repressed like his lips are sealed tight.

"Hey, baby," I breathe.

His breath hitches, and despite everything, my lips rise. Lashes drop. Peace washes through me, as slow and steady as a summer breeze.

But it's not lasting.

"Will."

Fuck.

His voice doesn't just crack, it breaks. Shatters into gasps. Like he's been holding his breath this whole time, and now that he finally released it, he can't keep up. He can't catch it.

"Easy," I say, instilling a calmness in my voice I'm one hundred percent faking. "You're okay. You're here, I'm here. The guys are with you. We're all good."

"You're not here," he says forcefully. I can practically feel the pressure of his teeth clenching through the words. "You're not fucking here."

Shit.

I sink back down on the bed. Elbows on my knees, I rub my jaw with the hand not holding the phone.

"No," I say tightly. My chest is on fucking fire. "I'm not *there*. But I'm here. Right here. Hear my voice?"

I picture him nodding jerkily as he croaks, "Not enough."

My knuckles rub against my sternum, trying to ease some of the building pressure. "No, but it's all we have right now."

He sucks in a choked breath.

I quickly change the subject, shifting it away from what we can't control, to what we can. Or rather, what *he* can. "Mason said you're at a diner."

"Yeah, finished up late."

When Waylon and I talked last night, they were just finishing up dinner and heading back to the studio to get a little more work in on their album. That was about four hours ago, give or take. I had just gotten upstairs after locking the bar up early for the night. Wednesdays are always pretty dead.

"What're you eating?" I ask, doing the math in my head. If it's a little after three a.m. here, it's only a little after midnight in LA.

"Waffles." He says it so grumpily, I have to stifle a laugh with my fist.

"Why do you sound pissed? Are they not good?" I ask, still smiling like an idiot. I'm sure if he was in the right state of mind he'd call me out for it.

"They *were...*"

I give a quick shake of my head, despite knowing he can't see it. "Nope. Forget about that. Did you drown them in syrup?"

"Obviously." He makes a sound of disgust. His voice is much steadier now as he says, "I think it's in my hair. I may've dove for cover face-first into the plate."

I roll my lips together. It shouldn't be funny, but it is.

"Shut up."

"I didn't say anything."

"Your face did."

Grinning, I shake my head, catching myself just before I remind him he can't see me.

"This is so fucking embarrassing," he grumbles, blowing out a breath, and I hear a shuffle. I picture him rubbing at his face, his eyes, like he usually does when coming out of a daze.

"Nah," I say easily. "I'm sure I would've done something even more embarrassing had I been there, like shove you under a table or something. Maybe threw the syrup bottle at Butter Finger's head."

He doesn't say anything to that. A heavy moment passes.

"Or maybe I would've shoved you," he finally says.

"Maybe." A beat. "But I'm quicker."

He groans.

"Stronger."

"Fuck. *Off.*"

I bite my lower lip, unable to contain my stupid ass grin.

"Shawn's looking at me weird."

Chuckling, I ask, "What kind of weird?"

"I don't know, but it's less weird than it was a moment ago. Now it's more like he wants to take the spoon he's holding, and scoop out my jugular."

I hum. "Something about that sentence doesn't sound right."

"Whatever. What are you doing?" His voice still sounds a little reedy, but I don't point it out.

Shaking my head, I say, "Sitting on my bed."

"Shit, it's like, what, the middle of the night over there?"

My mouth ticks up. "It's okay."

"Fuck," he mutters. "I'm sorry."

"Shut up."

He huffs.

"You good?"

A moment passes, before he says, "Yeah. Yeah, I'll be fine."

My teeth clench, and I feel the phone creak in my hand. The hard screen digging into my ear. "Say that again, and this time, make me believe it."

That gets a short laugh out of him, but I know better than to think that means everything's all roses and daisies now.

"I'm *fine*," he says, dragging out the word. I picture the barbell poking through his tongue flicking over his teeth, and *fuck me*, I should not be getting a boner right now.

But I miss him.

I miss him so much it steals my breath.

I miss him more than I ever thought possible.

"Just three more days," he whispers, and if I'm not mistaken, his voice has deepened, as if he senses where my thoughts have shifted.

"Three more days," I repeat robotically, staring vacantly around the bedroom, before landing on the ball of cotton on the floor next to the hamper.

Waylon's sweatshirt.

He threw it there the morning we came back from watching the sun rise on the bridge. Our last morning together. The rest of our clothes quickly found their way on the floor, too, but have since been put in the hamper. Normally, Waylon doesn't leave anything laying around—he's far neater than me—but in our rush to get to Philly once we realized we were late, he somehow overlooked his hoodie.

It hasn't moved from that spot in ten days. I just can't bring myself to pick it up.

And while there's only three days until I see his face again, there's still another month and a half, give or take, before he will notice his hoodie's still on the floor.

Fuck. This is harder than I thought.

"Will?"

I shake my head and force a hard swallow. "Sorry, did you say something?"

I can hear the grin in his voice. "No, you just got really quiet—"

My eyes roll, already knowing where this is going.

"—and you're never quiet."

"Har, fucking, har."

"I should go," he says, and I don't miss the exhaustion settling in, weighing down his words. This was far from being the worst panic attack he's ever had, but it's clear he's still zapped. "Mase just paid the bill. We gotta get back to the studio early."

"You think you'll be up for it?" I ask, not even bothering to hide my concern.

He sighs. "I have to be."

"Way—"

"Shut up, Mase," he says, making me think I'm not the only one calling him out. "It was just a little one. I'm fine now. We're already behind as it is, and I—"

Either Mason or Shawn must cut him off, but I can only hear muffled mumbling.

"Not if it means fucking you guys over," Waylon says, and I realize they're talking about this upcoming weekend, when I'm due to visit.

I already told him multiple times that I understood if he needed to work—that we'd still find time to be together. *Alone.*

But he was insistent.

"It's only two days, Will. Two fucking days. They can work around me. I'll just make sure I'm caught up on my parts so they don't need me."

I rolled my eyes at that. As if they could *not* need him.

But I know he meant recording. It's different from writing or practicing—when they're rehearsing with the sole intent to either perform, or to find their rhythm to hash out whatever might not be working.

Recording is a far more isolated process, apparently. It's just them, their instrument, or their voice, and the guy behind the glass barking orders at them.

Despite how much the guys didn't want to rely on machines to piece their music together, they kind of have to when it comes to slapping their songs on an album to be distributed to the masses.

"Babe, it's o—"

"It's fine," he cuts in quickly.

That's how many fines *now? Three?*

Shaking my head, I try again. "Way—"

"Look, I gotta go. They wanna clear the table."

"Are you—"

"I'm *fine*, Will," he says. There's a heaviness to his words now that wasn't there before. A pointedness, almost like he's pleading with me. To believe him. To drop it. To accept what we can't fucking change right now.

He's there.

I'm here.

Thousands of miles away from each other, with nothing but a phone line to tether us.

And all I can think is, *that's four.*

"I love you," I tell him, instead of what I want to say.

I'm not fine, Way. I'm not fucking fine, and neither are you, and this, right now, saying goodbye to you, knowing just how not fine you are, but not being able to see you, kiss you, touch you, and breathe you in...

It's straight up agony.

But I don't say any of that.

I just let those three little words slip into his ear, and silently pray the weight of them is enough to compensate for what I can't show right now. Not for three more whole fucking days.

Hearing his gulp in my ear, I know this is just as hard for him. But like me, he's trying to be strong. "I love you too. You'll call me in the morning?"

I smile thinly. "You know it."

After we say our too-quick byes, I let the phone drop to the bed next to me and bury my face in my hands.

The television is still playing in the living room, but the droning sounds of an infomercial ain't cutting it anymore.

The place feels like a tomb.

This room, this apartment...

The bar without them, without *him*...

I know some of it's in my head. These fears of mine, deep-seated with nowhere to go but further in. To places I can't even reach. Places I don't even know about until I get that *itch* and can't see anything outside of it.

Outside of what I need to do.

Muttering a curse, I grab my phone, pulling up my second recent contact.

It rings a couple times before I hear a click, then: "You better have a really, really fucking good reason why you're calling me in the middle of the night."

Cracking my knuckles against my knees, I say, "There's been a change of plans."

Ivy groans, but before I can say anything, she goes, "I swear on my cousin's life, if you don't get on that fucking plane this time, I will change all the locks and you'll have no fucking choice but—"

I hang up on her, shaking my head.

Guess that's all the permission I need.

Jumping to a stand, I head back to our dresser and start grabbing shit.

Three days.

Three fucking days.

In the grand scheme of things, three days is nothing.

Shoving clothes in my old duffle, I grab my phone and pop open the app I've been religiously scoping the last, well, ten days, and pull up the schedule for Delta Airlines.

They're gonna hate me there, I think dryly, hitting the *Confirm* button without hardly a glance before throwing on the first clean shirt I can find, and exchanging my sweats for jeans.

I flip the lights, shut off the television in the living room, and unplug the coffee pot before the timer can kick on.

Swinging my bag over my shoulder, I grab my keys and hightail it to the front door, locking up behind me without a backward glance.

Yeah, three days is a blink, but in the grand scheme of all that is near and dear and holy to *me...*

Fuck. That.

West Coast, here I come.

2

WAYLON MCALLISTER

TONIGHT'S GONNA BE A bad night.

Mason hits the lights, plunging the studio into black. He's the last one out of the room, so he locks up while Shawn and I start heading down the dimly lit hallway.

Digging out my pack of smokes from my back pocket, I slap them against my palm and focus on putting one foot in front of the other.

Faded red brick walls stretch out on either side of me as we pass by the other practice rooms, doors closed and already locked for the night.

The building is owned by Slater Records, the label we signed with to produce our first album, with their state of the art recording studio located three floors up.

Footsteps sound behind me, quick and loud before fading off as Mason catches up to us.

I try not to stiffen. I *know* it's him.

But there's something about this narrow fucking hallway and buzzing lightbulbs swinging from the ceilings that gives me the creeps.

And not in a fun way.

More like a trapped in a closet way.

There's a joke in there somewhere, and for a second the pressure in my chest eases as I think of Will.

I don't really think he'd appreciate the joke though, pun and all.

Too soon, he'd say. To which I'd say back, *When will it not be?*

I blow out a breath. In front of me, Shawn doesn't break stride as he flits me a quick look over his shoulder. He doesn't have to say anything. Neither do I.

Even Mason's silence closing in on me from behind speaks volumes.

STILL BEATING (PAPERBACK)

They know I'm losing my shit.

Hell, who am I kidding? I've been slowly losing my shit since our late-night dinner last night, when some fuckhead had to go and drop a frying pan as I was digging into my waffles.

The pack of cigarettes in my hand crinkles from the pressure of my fist, as I remember the echo of it slamming against the linoleum floors of the diner ringing out like a—

"Way."

"I'm fine," I say sharply. I don't even know who spoke.

Easy, a voice warns me, one that sounds suspiciously like the guy I'm trying really hard not to think about right now. Knowing it would only send me spiraling faster.

Blinking a few times, I wince against the grating buzz of another stupid, swinging lightbulb.

I mean, really, couldn't they've afforded something a little less garage chic?

My teeth clench and I stare hard over Shawn's shoulder, counting the steps I have left as the hallway ends, giving way to a small, but spacious, foyer. One with glass walls stretched out before me, giving me an unobstructed view of the outside world.

There, I think, cracking my neck as I step away from the guys, finally feeling like I can breathe again.

Me and tight spaces, we have a love-hate relationship these days. And today's not a day where I'm feeling the heart-eyes. Today's a day where I want to curl up in a ball and not exist for a couple hours.

I frown, steps slowing until I come to a stop inches from the double glass doors. "What time is it?"

Street lamps light up the quiet street. A car whooshes by, spraying puddle-water on the sidewalk. Heavy bass thrums from an old beater car idling in front of the apartment complex across the street, rattling the glass.

"A little after midnight," Shawn says, pushing open the door. He holds it for me, and I hold it for Mason as he trails behind us.

Shit, I think. *Another late night.*

We usually call it quits by nine, but we've been struggling with this one song the label wants on our album. To *diversify* it, whatever that means.

Because it's happier than the other tracks? I scoff at the thought.

Well, as it turns out tweaking happy music when I'm not exactly happy is really fucking hard. Shocking, right? Who knew?

It's only been ten days, a voice reminds me.

I mentally flip it off.

Tonight, though, tonight was about more than just figuring out why this song isn't working. Hell, even our agent, Paul, who usually never leaves our side when we're at the studio, left hours ago, knowing we were done getting anywhere. I only vaguely remember him slipping out with a tired, "See ya," leaving us to our guitars and notebooks and Mason's keyboard.

In the corner of my eye, I watch as Mason steps around me, snapping a photo with his phone of the semi-busy street.

I fight an eye roll. He's always taking pictures these days of the most random things. When I asked what that's about, all he said was, "Snapchat."

At first I thought he was posting them for our followers on the band's page. We don't have a crazy huge following, despite what it might look like on our TikTok page—that shit's very misleading, we've come to find out—but it's big enough.

Big enough to garner the attention of vicious assholes who want to shit on our success for no other reason than they *can*... or die-hard stalker types who want to have our babies.

So, yeah, I'd rather strangers on the internet *not* know where we are in real-time, thank you very much. Hence why I stay away from socials like my life literally depends on it.

But Mason assured me he wouldn't do that, not without our explicit permission, so I assume he just sends the pictures to Ivy. Maybe Jeremy. Maybe that girl he befriended during his last stint in rehab, the one he went on a date with a little while ago.

Who fucking knows? And I don't really fucking care so long as I don't have to worry about some crazy-ass fan pulling a knife on me.

Worse things have happened in my life, so I'm not one to scoff off the possibility, as unlikely as it may be. I'm a fucking trauma magnet, okay? Bad juju everywhere.

I groan as soon as the thought comes. "Fucking Phoebe," I mutter.

"What was that?" Shawn says stopping next to a parking meter.

Reaching up, I pinch my nose and shake my head. "Nothing."

"Alright, enough," Mason says loudly.

Slowly, I drop my hand back at my side and step back, turning slightly as Mason joins us. He shoves his phone in his back pocket, the buttons on his flannel pulling across his chest with his movements.

"It's not *nothing*, you're not *fine*. You haven't *been* fine all day."

I roll my eyes. "Mase—"

"Today was a bad day," he says, as if it's really that fucking simple. He crosses his arms, silently daring me to dispute it.

And it's gonna be an even worse night, I think tiredly, not for the first or second or third time.

I didn't sleep last night. Told the guys I did, when really I just snuck down to the hotel gym for a couple hours once I was sure they were asleep. Then I spent the early morning walking the streets, and pacing the beach. Went for a run...

Anything to keep myself away from the hotel bar.

Anything to keep me from calling Will and begging him to hop on a plane.

So I've been dreading this all day. Counting down the minutes to when I'd no longer be able to put off sleep. In a bed that's not mine. In a city as foreign to me as another planet. Alone.

It's been ten days since we arrived in LA.

Ten days, and while it hasn't always been *easy,* it hasn't been hard. Not until today.

Because I had my first panic attack in weeks last night, and it's the first one I had in over a year that I didn't have Will with me to talk me the fuck down.

I mean, sure, he *tried* to.

Okay, he did.

But a cold, hard phone against my ear isn't exactly the same as a soft pair of lips against my head. Or strong arms holding me tight.

Hearing him breathe means shit to nothing when I can't feel it on my cheek.

When I can't feel his heart thumping against my chest.

When I can't remember his dark blue eyes without picturing them red-rimmed with tears and wide with panic. Blood dripping down his temple. The smell of motor oil burning a pathway up my nose and down my throat.

"What do you need?"

At the sound of Shawn's voice, I'm pulled from my thoughts.

They're both standing in front of me now. Like a wall separating me from the world beyond. Or maybe like a wall to keep me in. I'm not sure if it's supposed to make me feel feral or safe.

Ping-ponging my gaze between them, I wonder what I'm supposed to say here. To give myself time, I quickly pull out a cigarette, light up, and inhale a long, scorching drag.

What do I need, what do I need...

Tipping my head back, I squint at the overcast sky as I blow out a cloud of smoke.

It's not like I can tell them the truth. The truth is fucking pathetic, and I'm trying really, really hard not to be pathetic.

It also doesn't take a shrink to tell me it's unhealthy too. I *know* it is. The problem is, though, if it's not Will I allow myself to need, it's—

"A fucking drink," I gravel out up at the starless sky, nose flaring as my eyes burn, throat searing.

I blink rapidly as my vision blurs. Dropping my head, I stare unseeingly at the spot between their shoulders. I feel more than see them share a loaded look.

"Well," Mason says slowly, "I for one could use an Oxy right about now. You know, something to take the edge off."

I still.

Shawn huffs, and my gaze snaps to him just as he runs a tanned hand through his dark hair. "Pretty sure that's a dealer standing over there." He jerks his head toward the right.

My eyes follow, to the corner across the street where a guy shuffles about, hood drawn over his head and hands in his pocket as he paces, face downturned.

"Saw him there the other night, slapping hands with a couple of scrawny ass kids."

Swallowing hard, I drag my gaze back to his.

Mason blows out a harsh breath. "And there's a bar. Two actually, right over there." He nods down the opposite way.

I know, I think, taking another drag from my cigarette. I already imagined all the ways I could sneak over there. The excuses I could come up with. Even reasoned with myself that I've cut back enough by now, that I can start fresh. Keep it under control. I know better now.

But it'll be a year sober in just under a month, and to be honest, it's that fact more than anything that's been keeping me from flushing it all down the drain. I want to hit that one-year mark.

After that though...

Shaking my head, I try not to think about it. Especially seeing as I won't be home with Will when that day inevitably comes.

I'll be here, in the City of Angels, with two other addicts who just proved how easy it would be to give in to our vices.

And here I was thinking it hasn't been on their mind at all. It's why I hadn't even been able to voice the words until now. Until it came down to blurting that or the fact I'm jonesing for my boyfriend.

See? Pathetic.

I didn't want to trigger them. So much for fucking that.

I swallow hard. "Don't..." My voice trails off, and I shake my head, unsure what I wanted to even say.

"Don't what? Talk about it?" Mason says.

In the corner of my eye, Shawn lights up a cigarette of his own. He's been trying to quit. I probably don't make it easy for him, since I'm not.

Now is definitely not the time for that. *Sorry, man.*

I meet Mason's light blue eyes.

His mouth ticks up, pulling at his lip ring. He shrugs. "It's what we're all thinking, right?" He glances at Shawn for confirmation, who nods, blowing out smoke from his nose, before continuing, "It's easy back home. We know who and what to avoid. We're comfortable. Our... need or whatever isn't so loud, because we're used to it there."

"And we're not used to anything here," Shawn finishes quietly.

Mason sounds pained when he says, "We could all give in. Easily. And maybe... maybe no one would know."

Shawn says, "It's just us out here, right?"

I look between them. "What? No. Are you serious right now?" I shake my head. "No. Absofuckinglutely not. No. *Fuck.*"

Whirling around, I ignore my crushed smokes and the lit cigarette in my other hand as I clasp the back of my head.

It's starting to rain again, just a light drizzle that prickles my forehead, dampening my exposed skin.

It's been raining on and off since this morning, which is apparently super unheard of in LA. Not sure if it's a good sign, or a bad sign, that out of the thirty-some days a year it rains in this city, we happened to be here for one of them.

We need to haul ass, or we're gonna have to grab a ride before the skies open up on us. The idea of confining myself in a car or bus right now, with no easy way out, is not really at the top of my list of things I want to do in the foreseeable future.

Mason and Shawn are quiet behind me as I pace. I feel like a caged tiger, which is stupid. It's not like I'm rooted to this spot. Open roads surround me, and yet the world is closing in.

Make it make sense to me.

I'm not really taking anything in as my eyes dart around the street. Slater Records is on a side-street, so it's not too heavy with foot-traffic. Especially at this time of night, even if it seems to be bustling farther down at the intersection.

I stare blankly at the couple jogging hand in hand across the crosswalk. It feels like there's a boulder sitting on my chest right now as it really sinks in just how easy it could be to give in without Will here. Without anyone here.

Reggie, Ivy, Dr. Wells...

Deacon, my sponsor. An older man I met at the Addicts Anonymous meetings I sometimes go to with Shawn and Mason back home.

I don't go often. Neither does Deacon. We met on a whim a few months back and hit it off right away. I'm his first sponsee, and he's my first sponsor. It's a match made in whiskey Heaven, sans the whiskey, something he gave up two years before I was even born. So he's basically a pro at this whole sober-livin' thing.

I know I could call him, or any one of my so-called support system, and they'd do what they can to talk me off the ledge in a heartbeat. Even if it's just to stay on the phone and listen to me bitch for as long as I can stay awake. They'd fucking do it, the masochists.

Hell, Will would probably steal a plane and fly himself to me if he could. Especially if he knew I lied this morning when I ignored his call, and sent him back a text with some bullshit excuse about how I couldn't talk because we were finally making good headway in the studio.

Spoiler alert: we did not make any kind of *way* today, because said *Way,* as in yours truly, kept fucking everything up. Losing count, losing focus, losing my patience...

Just all the losing, until ultimately I gave up, and just... played angry nonsense on my guitar until my fingers bled.

But I try not to think about any of that right now, least of all lying to Will, or the fact I haven't heard from him since. Because I know what he'd say if he knew where my head was really at right now. I know he'd be pissed that I'm keeping it from him.

But he deserves to have a life outside of worrying about me. He deserves to have a fucking break.

"The point is we could," Mason finally says, slowly, meaningfully, and it takes me a second to remember what we were talking about.

Right. Flinging ourselves off the proverbial wagon.

"We always know we can," he says. "How else do you think we manage to resist when it's thrown in our faces?"

My brow furrows as I slowly drop my hands to my sides and turn to face them once more. A long line of ash falls off my cigarette, but I hardly notice. *It's not cutting it tonight.*

"Ignoring that little voice," he goes on, still side-eying Shawn, "shoving it away, pretending that giving in isn't as easy as it is..." He turns his gaze on me. "It does us no favors. It'll just bite us in the ass later when it all comes to a head and we're at our lowest."

Shawn nods. "Over time it gets easier to ignore. It'll become less of a shout, and more of a passing whisper. So when it *does* pipe up, usually when we're not doing so hot, or when we least expect it..."

"We're strong enough to shove it away and move on with our day," Mason finishes.

I swallow tightly as tears burn the back of my eyes.

"It's not a crime to... daydream about it," he says after a moment. "And it's not always helpful, trust me, but it... makes it more manageable. In a convoluted way, maybe, but... yeah."

"It's our way of planning for the worst," Shawn clarifies in a steady voice. "We picture it all. Taking that hit, that sip... what we need to do to get it... how we might hide it..." His shoulders rise, then fall with his exhale. He lifts his cigarette to his mouth and takes a quick puff. "Then we think about what comes after. The shaking, the nausea. The agonizing pain…"

Mason's eyes redden. "Phoebe screaming and crying in my face, beating my chest."

Shawn tips his head. "That."

They share a quick look and I frown, wondering what that's about.

"Whatever you need to do to keep that fantasy from becoming a reality, do it," Mason says, leveling his gaze with mine. "Use it. Find what works and don't be ashamed of it. Trust me, we all have our little anchors to hold on to when we feel ourselves drifting. It could be anything." He pauses meaningfully. "Including people."

"Yeah?" I perk up, my voice shaky. *Then why does it feel so wrong?*

He gives me a knowing smile. "You're one of mine."

My jaw quivers, and my eyes are on fire. "What? Why? That's…" I shake my head. I want to say that's stupid, but…

"Let's just say, the idea of seeing you spiral because *I* spiraled doesn't sit well with me."

"Ditto," Shawn says quietly.

My gaze snaps to his, wide with surprise.

And it suddenly occurs to me, we never really considered what he went through last year. Not only when Mason relapsed, but when I ghosted everyone for those couple weeks.

Shawn had Phoebe, I suppose. And Will. Ivy, too, when she wasn't with me.

So I guess he found other anchors.

But still...

I didn't think about how triggering all of that might have been for *him*.

"Why do you think we chose to be each other's sponsors?" Shawn says dryly, gesturing between him and Mason with his cigarette. "Because sometimes, the only thing that keeps us holding on, is holding on for someone else."

"The curse of being an addict," Mason says in an equally dry voice. "But also, maybe, our superpower."

Shawn grunts at that.

"But you're not each other's sponsors any more," I point out. "Remember?"

Mason nods. "Yeah, 'cause I fucked up," he says at the same time Shawn says, "Because I wasn't enough."

Mason and I both still.

"Shawn," Mason starts to say, turning toward him.

But he holds up a hand, looking at both of us. "It's okay." His mouth even ticks up in a smile, which says a lot. The dude never smiles.

STILL BEATING (PAPERBACK)

Still, I feel my brows furrowing low over my eyes as a frown pulls at my face. I take a long inhale from my smoke.

I didn't like how easily he said that, I realize. That he wasn't enough. That it's *okay.*

"That time," he says pointedly, "I wasn't enough."

But that's not what you said, I want to say. But like always with him, something stops me.

"Nothing was enough to hold me back," Mason grits out, pain and frustration evident in his voice.

I think back to what he said about his sister earlier. Using the memory of when she found him, after he overdosed.

Giving him a considering once-over, I blow smoke from the corner of my lips. "You never did tell us..."

I notice Shawn's watching him too, confirming my suspicions. He doesn't know why Mason broke his sobriety last year either; what triggered that whole breakdown he had.

I hate that I feel... relieved at that. That Shawn's just as in the dark as me.

Mason just shakes his head. "It was building up for a while."

My eyes narrow, because he's not looking at either of us when he says it.

Mason's always been a shit liar, ever since we were kids. He's got tells louder than his angry fists.

I just can't figure out *why* he's lying. It's not like saying it's 'cause of Izzy would be anything new and groundbreaking.

We already know that was definitely part of it, if not a huge fucking chunk.

Which means...

Whatever finally sent him over the edge didn't have to do with her.

Fuck, was it my fault?

"Point is," Mason goes on with a little huff, "we gotta talk about this shit. We can't pretend any of this is easy, because the fucking second we let down our guards, is the moment temptation will strike and we won't be strong enough to say no." He gulps and looks away, somewhere off in the distance. "We gotta rely on each other, and trust that we'll keep each other standing."

Shawn nods, tossing the cigarette butt to the ground, and stubbing it with his boot. "Now more than ever."

I look at him, then Mason, hearing what we're all probably thinking.

Because here in LA, all we have is each other.

Following Shawn's lead, I drop what's left of my cigarette, and ground out the cherry with my shoe.

"You're not gonna make us relapse, Way," Mason says gently. "Trust me, we're already thinking about it. Our heads are already there. You can talk to us, and... and we'll talk to you. We just... we weren't sure where *your* head's been at, so we wanted to give you a chance to bring it up yourself first."

Nodding, I swallow thickly and finally manage to say, "I get that." A beat, then: "Thank you."

Mason gives me a funny look and I just shake my head, shrug, not really sure where that came from, or what it means.

He rolls his eyes, steps forward, and throws an arm over my shoulders.

I try to shake him off, but he just squeezes me to him tighter. "No one's hitting up any bars, or slapping hands with some random fucker on the street," he says with a low chuckle. "We've got you, man. Whatever you need."

"It's a bad night," I utter. I still want to drink. I still want Will more than anything else. But I guess I don't feel as... alone or pathetic about it all.

"Yeah. It is."

"But tomorrow should be better," Shawn says quietly, voice heavy with some unnamed... something.

I feel my face bunch. *Will it though?* He sounds far too certain for my liking.

My gaze meets his, and something there gives me pause. But he's too quick to look away for me to try and figure out what it is.

"Definitely gonna be a better weekend," Mason says in a sly voice, yanking me out of my thoughts when he messes up my hair.

I side-eye him with a glare as I finally manage to shove him off. "Shut up."

I pat down my hair just as the rain starts to pick up.

"Fuck, we're gonna get soaked," Mason says, not sounding too put out about it. He starts walking in the direction of the hotel we're staying at. It's only a couple blocks, but...

"We can Uber," I suggest, jogging to catch up with him. *Please say no, please say no.*

He cuts me a look over his shoulder just as Shawn and I reach him. "Why would we do that?"

Shawn and I share a glance and a shrug.

"We're in Cali, baby!" Mason yells out suddenly at the top of his lungs. He tips his head back and howls. Spreading his arms out, he lets the rain beat down on his heaving chest. Soaking through his thin white shirt.

Someone whistles from nearby, just as a car whooshes by, splashing dirty ass water over the three of us.

Shawn curses as Mason lets out another obnoxious howl and I'm laughing. I'm smiling so big, it feels like my face might split.

My throat still feels thick, and it still feels like something heavy's sitting on my chest, but it no longer feels like an *I might die* kind of pressure.

More like an *I'm alive* kind of pressure.

It's a feeling I'm still getting used to. As is the emotional whiplash that comes from hurtling between the two at any given moment.

Something tells me I won't have to be alone tonight after all, even if it means they're exhausted tomorrow. I have to let them be there for me, just like I would for either of them.

By the time we reach the street our hotel's on, Mason and I are both belting the lyrics to "Under the Bridge" at the top of our lungs. No one we pass seems to mind. Hell, I think a couple people even had their phones out, recording us. We sound good, I know we do, even if we're choking on laughter through most of it.

They probably think we're drunk off our asses and I can't find it in me to care at the moment. We're a goddamn cliché set against the backdrop of Tinseltown, and *fuck,* I'm happy to be alive despite missing Will.

Shawn's shaking his head at us, but I don't miss the smile he's fighting tooth and goddamn nail to hold back.

Mason skips ahead as the lights of the valet entrance draw closer, welcoming us home.

I turn around, strutting backward as I press my hand to my chest and serenade Shawn about the city who loves me.

I don't realize Mason's stopped singing, much less that he's come to a stop. Nor do I immediately register Shawn's smile dimming, brown eyes widening on something behind me.

Not until it's too late and I crash into Mason's back.

My singing cuts off with an *oomph* and a bark of laughter. "Dude."

It's pouring now. Rain's splattering over my head and down my cheeks. My hair has been flattened, and dark pieces cling to my temples and the back of my neck.

I'm still smiling, still breathless, using Mason's shoulder as leverage to turn around so I don't fall over as I catch my balance.

"What—"

Only I never get a chance to ask. Not that I need to.

I was wrong before, I realize, as the figure huddled under the overhang comes into view.

So, so wrong.

I watch, drenched and frozen, as he pushes off the bench, coming to a stand.

Black t-shirt. Ripped jeans that look a little too tight to be his.

Dark blond hair mussed up every which way, and stubble lining his rigid jaw.

Knuckles white around the strap of the duffle he hikes up his shoulder. Biceps bulging, flexing with his movements and the tension lining his body.

His eyes are on mine, and mine are on his, and the whole damn city of Los Angeles could be burning right now for all I know.

Now, I think. *Now* I'm happy.

Not just happy, but *relieved.* Relieved I never gave up, never gave in, just so I could get to this moment. Right. Fucking. Here.

My eyes are burning, and I'm sure they're bloodshot to all hell. I can't smile, can't swallow. I don't so much as blink or breathe, too fucking terrified he might disappear if I do anything but *stare.*

He came.

Head empty of everything but that.

He came, he came, he came.

Well.

That is, until he opens his big, stupid, sexy mouth and ruins everything.

"Is he drunk?"

3

WAYLON MCALLISTER

At first, I'm pissed.

Like, really, really pissed.

Something dark and cruel rockets up my throat. I can feel my airway closing just behind it, telling me there will be no taking back whatever it is that comes out.

"Is he drunk?"

His question tumbles around my skull like one of those medieval weapons with the spike ball attached to a chain. The words are cutting, sharp and grating as they seem to tear at every good feeling I finally, *finally* managed to find after a day from *Hell.*

Irrational? Probably.

But again. Day from Hell. Not really feeling *rational* right now.

The irony doesn't escape me that if I *were* in fact drunk, as he just so rudely asked the guys—as if I'm not standing right fucking here—I probably wouldn't have been able to stop myself. Catch myself from saying or doing something unforgivable.

And if that's not a straight kick to the solar plexus, I don't know what it is.

It's my sobriety that probably just saved our relationship.

And that's a, ah, well, sobering thought.

"Way..." Mason warns quietly from my side. I'm sure I look about two seconds from blowing my lid.

I feel Shawn near my back just as he says quickly, "He's not. He didn't drink."

I grit my teeth, nose flaring.

Will shuffles in place ten feet away, the closest he's been in *ten fucking days,* and I'm over here, absolutely fucking seething.

That is, until I realize what stopped me from said blowing of my lid. Somehow under the red haze of my anger, my

STILL BEATING (PAPERBACK)

subconscious must've picked up on what I was too fucking blinded to see, and only now do I realize his question was not, in fact, an accusation.

He's not angry. Not disappointed.

He's fucking heartbroken.

Scared.

It just takes Shawn assuring him for it to fucking click in my head.

It just takes him crumbling for me to wilt completely.

"No," I hear myself rasp, just as I take a step forward, then another, and another. Not taking my eyes off his, I shake my head. "No."

The bag drops at his side with a thud.

"I didn't drink," I tell him, my voice breaking.

His face crumples just as I grab his shoulders and yank him into my arms.

"I didn't drink," I whisper into the roaring rain and whooshing static of LA nightlife.

His hair is dry, unlike mine. Clothes too, but not for long.

Water is dripping down on our heads from above. Rain's blowing into my back, and again, I can't help but think, *it never rains in LA.* Like that fact holds more meaning now.

Will's cheek is hot and wet against mine, and I hold him tighter to me, knowing the rain hasn't touched him there.

"I'm sorry," he chokes out.

His arms come under mine, sliding around my back, gripping me so tightly it should hurt. It doesn't.

He's here.

"This wasn't part of the plan," I croak. I try to pull back and grab his cheeks to look at him, but he buries his face into my neck, preventing me.

My eyes widen and I look over my shoulder, seeking my two suspiciously quiet best friends out, silently begging them for some sort of guidance here.

My boyfriend is fucking falling apart in my arms right now and I have no idea what to do.

Fuck, did something happen to his parents?

"Will," I breathe, glancing down at him. But I don't think he hears me. "Did something happen?"

He just holds me tighter.

Okay then.

I don't think he's outright crying. It's more like he's trying really, really fucking hard to hold it together. Like he's imploding into himself, and he's using me as a shield to keep it all contained.

"Did you know he was coming?" I ask in a hush, looking at Mason first.

He shakes his head, eyes wide like he's just as shocked as me. "I texted him this morning."

My gaze snaps to Shawn. But he's not looking at me. He's looking at the guy in my arms, brows pinched in something akin to concern.

Will says something, but it's too muffled for me to make out.

Turning, I dip my head lower. "Say that again."

A throat clears, and I feel his swallow against my neck just before he pulls back. He doesn't look up at me, just stares at some spot on my chest.

"I was already on my way."

I still.

His shoulders hunch slightly, and I can just make out the muscles of his jaw working. "Got held up in Chicago. Got here as fast as I could. Phone died..."

My eyes burn as what he's telling me fully registers.

"You didn't have to do that," I whisper before I can think better of it.

He flinches.

Shit.

Looking around, I only now realize there are people around. Not a lot, not with it being this late, but a good handful.

Some eyes drift our way, but not in disgust. Just curiosity, maybe. Probably wondering why these two boys are hanging on to each other in the rain for dear life.

My pulse speeds up and I feel my fingers biting into Will's arms, but I don't think he notices. Not when he's too busy trying to extract himself from my hold.

I snap my gaze to his face, but he still won't look at me.

"Hey," Mason says, approaching me. His hand brushes my shoulder and he turns so his mouth's near my ear. "We're gonna go grab a bite since we didn't eat dinner. Why don't you guys go upstairs?"

He slips me his copy of the keycard, knowing I forgot mine as usual.

Will turns away from me, bending down to get his bag. Hoisting it over his back like it's the heaviest thing in the world.

He's still carefully avoiding my gaze.

Mason tries to give me a reassuring smile when I turn to him, but it falls flat. "If you need us, just call. Okay?"

My stomach cramps.

It's not me you should be worried about, I want to tell him.

But I get it. I'm the addict here, not Will.

I'm the one with a history of suicidal tendencies, not Will.

Bitterness rears up its ugly, foul head.

Will matters too.

Shawn draws near, eyes still trained over my shoulder, before finally finding mine.

44

"You asked him to come," I say quietly, my voice shaking with some emotion I can't place. I'm hoping Will doesn't hear me. I don't want him to think I'm mad.

Shawn doesn't so much as bat an eye. "You needed him."

My molars grind and I feel my nostrils flare.

Mason turns away, sliding his phone out from his back pocket as he gives us a moment.

"It's better to need someone than to have no one to need," Shawn says, his fierce gaze holding mine. "Trust me."

My eyes burn as all I can do is stare unblinkingly at him.

He lets out a little sigh, nods, and goes to turn around.

Before I can think better of it or second-guess myself, I reach out and grab the hem of his shirt, taking care not to touch *him*.

He can touch you, but you can't touch him. That is the rule.

Halting mid-step, his shoulders bunch.

Holding my breath, I wait.

Finally, he turns his head just enough to look down at the arm extending toward him.

His gaze tracks it up to my face, eyes swirling with something dark I've only seen glimpses of.

"You're enough for me," I tell him roughly.

His eyes widen a fraction.

With that, I let go, step back and nod.

Partially in thanks, partially in promise.

Something seems to splinter in his gaze when he realizes what I mean, but he quickly looks away, shutting me out.

I watch as he jogs over to where Mason smiles down at his phone.

Inhaling deeply, I turn away from them to find Will watching me.

There you are, I think, pressing my lips together in a tight smile.

"Come on," I say.

And not giving him a chance to stop me, I quickly tug the duffel bag off his shoulder, throw it over mine, grab his hand, and head for the doors.

He's here, I think.

That's all that matters in this second.

The rest is just noise.

4

WILL FOSTER

MY BOOTS SQUEAK ACROSS the linoleum floors of the hotel lobby as Waylon all but drags me past the front desk, past the lounge, past the empty luggage carriers parked against the wall.

It's late, but people still linger about. A group of businessmen are checking in at the desk, and a couple of them look our way with a frown when they hear the squelch of our fast-paced footsteps treading rain water across the lobby.

But Waylon doesn't seem to notice, or care.

His head's trained forward, eyes locked on some unseen destination, and I can't help but notice how *wet* he is.

Or how wet I am after hugging him so hard I'm pretty sure I left bruises.

I should feel worse about that, but frankly I'm just too spent to care about anything other than the fact he's holding my hand.

In public.

Not for the first time, no, he did that in Philly months ago, but it still matters. It still means something. It will always mean something.

Hell, it means even more to me in this moment than it did then, because this isn't a Pride parade. This isn't him trembling and sweaty, squeezing my hand so tight my fingers grind as he stares wildly around at everyone, trying not to panic.

This is a Waylon on a mission.

Strong, steady, determined.

A force to be reckoned with for all the world to fucking see and damn anyone who has anything less than nice to say about it.

Music filters out of the overhead speakers once we reach a short hallway. Elvis crooning about missing his love. Fitting, I suppose, minus the whole *ex-lover* aspect.

Not so lonesome now, are we though? a voice remarks dryly.

Waylon turns, leading us to a row of elevators. It's an old hotel, I notice, nothing too fancy, but clean.

Without letting go of me, he uses his other hand to jab at the button a couple times, before hiking the bag up his shoulder when it starts to droop.

"I could carry that, you know." Fuck, my voice sounds flat and exhausted even to my own ears.

He stiffens.

I feel more than hear his inhale, but before he can say anything, the elevator dings and the doors open. A lady walks out, not lifting her gaze from her phone as she easily side-steps us.

Waylon's hand tightens around mine, but then we're in the elevator and the breath is whooshing out of him.

The doors close. He hits a button.

Everything's happening so fast.

"Fuck," he grits out.

Staring at his profile, I take in the lines around his eyes as they dart rapidly back and forth over the numbers lighting up above the door.

I swear he's holding his breath.

Fortunately, we only have to go up five floors and not the sixteen this hotel holds.

He had a panic attack last night, a voice reminds me.

Jesus Christ, has it really only been twenty-four hours?

Stepping closer to him, I bump his shoulder with mine. In nothing but a gray t-shirt soaked all the way through, he might as well be naked.

I take in his wet, inky black hair. The droplets of rain streaking down his smooth, sculpted cheeks, and clinging to thick dark lashes.

The pulse fluttering under his clenched jaw, and the purse of his normally full lips.

Fuck, this boy is beautiful.

I bump his shoulder again.

He snaps his head around, hazel eyes clashing with mine.

"Hey," I whisper.

His eyes drop to my mouth, and he swallows with an audible click

Ding!

We separate like we're going to be caught doing something—save for our hands, which I'm pretty sure he's somehow welded together. It's absurd. It's all absurd. Unlike downstairs, no one's around anyway, once we step out into the hall.

We pass by one door, two doors, then, finally, he slows to a stop. *Room 504.*

I was already up here a little over an hour ago. But no one answered.

STILL BEATING (PAPERBACK)

The panic I felt earlier when I realized they weren't here makes a brief reappearance.

They worked late last night, I remember thinking. *Today was supposed to be an early day.*

And when I went back down and asked the man at the front desk where they may have gone, and he told me *"I don't know, kid. Probably a bar,"* like it was nothing at all, I just—

I lost it.

My phone was dead. I forgot to pack a charger because I rushed out of the apartment like an idiot. Shawn knew I was coming sometime tonight, but didn't know when.

I was exhausted, having run on nothing more than a couple hours of fitful sleep. Exhausted from the never-ending flight, the never-ending layover, the never-ending day because of the change in time zones that made it feel like I was getting *farther* away from Waylon, rather than closer.

It was all too much.

It's all *been* too much.

And here Waylon thought he'd be the weak one. The one who'd break.

I barely notice as he slides the card in the slot. The door seems to exhale as he unlocks it and pushes it open.

I already know what the room looks like, having seen it on a shaky FaceTime video when they first arrived. Waylon's wide, dimpled grin, and his green-gold eyes lit up like a little kid's as he checked out each room in their joined suite, forever ingrained in my memory.

It's all paid for by the record company, of course. Well, with the addendum that the Lost Boys make them money in return. Nothing actually comes free in this industry.

The heavy door slowly closes behind us with a click as it automatically locks.

Waylon doesn't break stride as he tosses the keycard on a table, dragging me by the hand past the first closed door.

He throws open the next one, drops my bag on the floor and turns, grabbing me by the shoulders and guiding me toward the bed.

"Sit," he says, giving me a little push.

The bed is freshly made, telling me the cleaning lady has been through. That or Waylon is the type of guy to make a hotel bed every morning.

Frowning, I backtrack. Actually, he totally *is* the type of person to make a hotel bed every morning.

Hands reach for my shirt, fingers twisting in the fabric as he starts pulling it off my body.

Looking up at him, I'm not quite sure what this weird feeling is sitting in my chest.

It only grows stronger when he steps back, hardly even looking at my bare chest as he sinks to the ground and gets to work on unlacing my boots.

His movements are almost rushed, not quite shaky in a scared way, but jittery in a way that tells me he's impatient.

And while normally him stripping me down like this would be a total fucking turn-on, sex feels like the *last* thing on our minds right now.

Once he's got my shoes off, he begins working on my belt and fly. My hands come up on top of his, pausing his movements just as he gets the top button undone.

Our gazes crash into one another's.

"What are you doing?" I ask him.

Waylon's throat bobs with a swallow. "I'm taking care of you." The words wrench out of him slow and deep. The power in such a simple sentence would send me to my knees if I wasn't already on my ass.

He releases his hold on my jeans, pushes past my slack arms, and raises his fingers to my cheeks. They're rough with callouses. Pretty sure I saw dried blood on them before.

But I don't care, because he's touching me, stroking the paper-thin skin under my eyes and watching me with such a soft look of adoration, I don't know how my heart's still in my chest, and not at his feet.

"You haven't been sleeping," he says.

I clutch my fingers in my hand. "Neither have you."

"This wasn't part of the plan," he says slowly, carefully. Yet emotion still breaks through, thrumming his words. "Three more days."

My eyes burn as I clamp down on my molars.

"I was gonna pick you up at the airport," Waylon says, his voice finally breaking. "We had a plan. We could do this."

I'm shaking my head. *Who cares?* I want to say. *Who cares?*

"They shouldn't have called you," he says in a resigned voice. His fingers fall from my face at the same time my gut falls to the floor.

What?

He pushes to a stand and turns around, clasping the back of his head. Wet dark strands of hair slipping through his inked knuckles.

I force a hard swallow. "Should I not have come?"

He freezes.

Slowly, *slowly*, his hands drop to his sides and he turns around. Shaking his head, he starts to say, "What—"

I stare through him. "Am I making it worse?"

A heavy beat passes where it's so quiet, there's no possible way he can't hear the pulse pounding in my ears.

He was laughing, I think, remembering when I first saw him tonight. He was laughing and smiling and singing...

And I thought he was drunk.

STILL BEATING (PAPERBACK)

Because I didn't see how he could possibly be happy after what happened in the diner—after I spent the day in agonizing worry over what I'd be walking into once I got here.

Imagining the worst...

I squeeze my eyes shut as the reality of what happened finally sinks in.

I underestimated him.

I fucked up.

I let old ghosts win.

"Baby."

My shoulders tense. Pretty sure my heart tenses too, if that's even possible.

My lashes flutter open to find Waylon watching me with tear-filled eyes. He's not quite smiling, but his dimples are out, sinking deep into his cheeks.

"Baby," he says again, this time so much deeper, and then he's crawling into my lap.

He doesn't call me that often. He's not one to use cutesy pet names, not like me, who will call him every cutesy name in the book.

He pretends to hate it, but he doesn't fool me.

So when *he* does it, especially when he calls me *that*, it feels like a weapon. One forged specifically to make me shatter. Make me melt.

Hands clutch my face as jean-clad knees come down on either side of my hips. He's not much smaller than me, so it's awkward, but perfect, as his ass sits back on my knees.

Lifting my face to his, I guide his rain-stained lips to mine.

He sighs—or maybe it's me. Maybe it's both of us as our tongues push feverishly into each other's mouths.

His fingers move into my hair, tugging, while my hands move to his back, gripping.

Arching into me, his hard chest slides up against mine. I'm shirtless, he's not, but he might as well be.

He's all damp cotton and slick, steamy skin. All desperate fingers and grinding hips and if he doesn't get naked soon I'm going to explode.

"You're here," he pants, his fingertips finding my cheeks once more, trembling over my stubble.

"I'm here," I say, my voice breaking, as I wrap my arms fully around his back, holding him impossibly tighter.

"God, I've missed you," he growls into my mouth before biting down on my lower lip.

A grunt punches out of me as I reach up, fork my fingers in his hair, and wrench his head back.

Waylon's lashes flutter up at the ceiling. Mouth agape.

So much for sex being the last thing on our minds.

Then again, we've always been better at combusting first and reasoning with ourselves later.

I lean forward and press a soft kiss to his throat, just under his Adam's apple. His whole body seems to shrink then expand with his exhale, tattoos and muscles rippling across his body.

"You need sleep," he says to the ceiling, voice strained.

I rub my nose back and forth over his jaw. "I need you," I utter thickly.

He gives a stilted nod. "Have me."

And with that, I lurch up with all the strength I've been conserving these last torturous twenty-some hours, gripping his ass in one hand, his hair in the other, so as not to let go of him.

Sucking in a startled breath, he then sinks into me as he slides down my body. As soon as his feet are on the ground, I'm attacking his mouth with mine.

"I-I need a shower," he manages to gasp out as I pull back just enough to peel the shirt off his body.

Jesus Christ.

His chest is heaving. Stomach muscles clenching. Tattoos decorate nearly his whole torso, arms, and creep up the side of his neck.

The barbell poking through his nipple looks brighter than fucking ever against his skin, making me realize he's got a bit of a tan since being in LA.

"God, I could eat you," I say into a groan as I drop my face to his shoulder. I open my mouth, nibbling at his flesh. He tastes like sweat and rain water, dirty but *mine.*

His chuckle is low and wicked as he strokes a hand up my back. The other drops to my ass, pulling me against him.

"Shower first," he croons into my ear.

I press my teeth a little deeper in him. "Fine."

We grind up against each other one last time for good measure, and then he's pulling away, walking backward as he starts undoing his belt.

I rub a thumb over my bottom lip, watching him, not taking my eyes off his body as he slowly strips down to nothing.

"You just gonna stand there and gawk, City Boy," he drawls, kicking away the last article of clothing, "or are you gonna make good on that promise you made me the other day?"

My gaze flashes up to his, mouth drying as I remember what we talked about on the phone the other day. All the plans we made for this coming weekend....

His cock is hard and long, jutting out at me obscenely, beckoning me.

My mouth ticks up and I shake my head.

I know I need to sleep.

Know we need to talk.

Know our growing issue of long-distance relationshipping is far from solved.

But right now...

Right now I'm gonna make my cocky, stubborn-ass boyfriend forget his own name.

5

WAYLON MCALLISTER

WE CRASH INTO THE bathroom in a tangle of limbs.

It's the only one in the suite, and I send a silent thank you to the guys for being so cool about this. It's late and they've gotta be exhausted after a long day of playing music without really getting anywhere. I'm sure they would've just skipped food and went straight to bed if Will hadn't shown up.

But instead, they gave me this.

Will's here.

He came, he came, he came.

Right when I needed him most.

Firm fingers grip my waist, using me for balance as he hobbles to reach one hand back, then the other, to yank off his socks. I shove his jeans and boxers down once he's steady, and he wastes no time in shucking them off completely, before plastering himself to me. Fully naked.

His bare cock brushes against mine, before pressing against my stomach like a heavy, hot brand. I cup his ass, squeezing him, pulling a deep groan from his chest as I grind my hard length up against his.

Our tongues swirl hotly in his mouth, and then I'm pulling back, scraping my teeth over his lip. He tastes like rain water and something headier, something distinctly *Will.*

He makes a small noise of protest as I arch away from him, reaching blindly around me for the shower knobs.

It's a massive walk-in shower, with one of those fancy rectangular showerheads that take up almost the entire stall. Feels like you're in a rainstorm. It's fucking Heaven.

Hands spread widely over my lower back, the sides of his pinkie fingers teasing the slope of my clenched ass.

"Damn," Will breathes, pressing a quick kiss to my shoulder. His pupils are blown, eyes heavy with arousal as he takes in the shower behind me. "This is some fancy ass shit you got here."

STILL BEATING (PAPERBACK)

The pipes creak the slightest bit, and then water comes cascading down, crashing onto the tiled flooring. I hum a kiss against his cheek, before turning away to adjust the temperature.

Big wall to wall mirrors surround the shower from the waist up, so I have a perfect, unobstructed view of Will standing behind me. Tall and tanned. Muscular shoulders bunched from holding me so tight.

Like he's terrified to let me go.

Like I might disappear if he does.

Our gazes connect in the mirror, and I'm thrown back to the many times we met like this.

That first night, over a year ago, in a dingy bar bathroom. A girl caught between us, none the wiser to the storm brewing around her.

Then months later, when he held me back from punching out my reflection. The night I thought we might never come back from.

The club bathroom, confetti and glitter sticking to our temples. Chests heaving. Lips still tingling. His raw confession— *"You are loved. And I'm not better off without you."* —and the heartbreak that followed...

"We're not good for each other, Waylon. Not like this."

"We have a lot of moments in bathrooms, don't we?" I whisper, chest growing heavy from the memories of our rocky start.

His mouth lifts at the corners. "You noticed that too?"

I laugh and it's creaky.

His features soften and he drops his mouth to the side of my head. "No regrets."

Sliding my eyes shut, I nod. "No regrets." *But I'm still sorry.*

Steam fills the room, tickling my skin. The heat beckons, even though I'm already boiling.

As if reading my mind, Will slides his hands to my hips, and gives me a little nudge to get under the spray.

I hear the glass door slide shut just as I whirl around, grab Will by the skull, and crush his mouth to mine in an open, messy kiss. His arms come around me, catching me, just before we would've gone tumbling into the doors.

The water pounds down on our faces and slides over our shoulders. We're pressed so tightly together, water pools along the grooves of our collarbones.

"Fuck," he mutters, sucking water off my bottom lip.

He pulls back, cupping my cheeks in his warm palms. I blink through the water sliding down my head, my temples, droplets clinging heavily to my lashes. He collects the ones that fall with his fingers.

Moving his palm, Will drags a thumb over my lips, and I pull the warm digit in, hollowing my cheeks as I suck him over my tongue.

His face bunches like he's in pain, and the fingers still clutching my side press harder. So hard, I feel his nails digging into my skin.

"Goddamn," he breathes, eyes darkening. He bows his forehead to mine, rocking it back and forth. His knuckles and the thumb in my mouth are all that separate our lips as we just breathe, in and out, in and out, sharing air. "You're killing me."

He removes his thumb from my mouth and crushes his lips to mine in a sweltering kiss.

Time loses all sense of meaning as we map each other's naked bodies with our hands, re-memorizing anything we might've forgotten in the time we spent apart.

Eventually our kisses ease into something lighter, something more playful as we grab the soap and finally make work of washing off the day.

My dick is still so fucking hard, as is his, so we don't dally, or worry about making some sensual thing of it. We both know where this is headed.

Back home, we showered together more often than not, so it's long since stopped being awkward. It's just two people getting clean together. Routine. Methodical. Perfectly mundane.

Intimate in the purest sense of the word. Boners and all.

At one point, I throw the loofah I was using at his chest. Will grabs my wrist, tugging me to him with a growl that breaks a low laugh out of me. We're all jabbing elbows and soapy fingers and not-so-secret looks as we fight for the shampoo.

It's insane.

Loving him this easily...

Like every piece of me was made for every piece of him.

He adds a big blob of shampoo to my hair before pouring some out into his palm to run through his own hair.

Watching him now, it's hard to believe it was just an hour ago, not even, that I was losing my shit on the side-streets of LA.

When he's here, in reaching distance, it doesn't feel so pathetic to want him, need him, *breathe* for him.

My mind plays back what happened outside the hotel as my eyes catch once more on the shadows under his eyes.

I've seen Will upset and scared before, but this time, it hits different. I'm not really sure why. Maybe because we hadn't seen each other in ten days. Maybe because I had it all planned out in my head how I would greet him in the airport.

Maybe because for a second, even before he spoke, I was furious he jumped on a plane, days earlier than scheduled, all because I had a stupid panic attack.

I was ashamed. Still kind of am, to be honest.

Hanging my head, I wash the shampoo out of my hair.

Later, I tell myself. I'll deal with all that later.

What matters is he's here now. Naked and soapy and too fucking gorgeous to be real.

After rinsing out the suds from my hair, I step forward and press my hands to his chest, smoothing my fingers over his hard muscles. His heart thumps steadily against my palm. Nipples pebbling between my fingers.

Nope, definitely real. Yet impossibly all mine.

I watch through slitted eyes as he tips his head back, letting the water cascade down his face. He runs his fingers through his wet hair, washing out the soap, before slicking it back.

Stepping even closer, I press my nose to his stubbly jaw, and slide my eyes shut against the water beating down from above.

Big, strong hands come around my back as a mouth feathers across my temple. "Done?"

I hum, nodding as I rub my nose all up in his soapy, wet skin. He smells like me now, like my soap.

His fingers find the back of my head, much gentler now than they were before as he cradles my head, pulling it back just enough to bump noses. Then lips.

He flicks his tongue out, before replacing it with his teeth. He gives my bottom lip one last tug, then pulls back with that crooked, infuriating grin of his. "Turn around," he orders deeply.

Heat explodes across my cheeks but I do as he says.

At first I freeze when I come face to face with my reflection. It's not as clear as it was, thanks to the steam and water droplets streaking down the surface, but still clear enough to see my hooded, dark eyes staring back at me. The flushed cheeks. The parted lips.

It's nerve-wracking and hot all at once.

Hands come around my waist, giving me a little shove forward.

Not expecting it, I throw my arms out, slamming my palms against the mirror.

"Good boy."

Fucking. Christ.

I watch through wide eyes as he drops down behind me. His knees are bent between mine as he balances on the soles of his feet. Hands clutching my ass for leverage.

Warm, slick hands stroke over my cheeks. "God, I've missed this ass. Maybe even more than who it belongs to."

That startles a choked laugh from me. My knuckles push against my skin as I dig my bruised fingertips into the mirror. "You're such a dic—"

My words cut out with a sharp hitch of air as I feel his teeth clamp down on my ass.

"Be nice," he says softly, before flicking his tongue over my skin to soothe the ache.

His words echo all around me, and I shudder, dropping my forehead to the mirror. He squeezes my bottom, moving his lips toward my crease as he spreads me.

And all I can think is, *thank God the guys aren't here.* Because not a moment later, I feel warm, wet heat right over my hole, ripping a sound from me that I can't even be sure is human. Caught somewhere between a whimper and a moan, it fills the room, clashing with the rush of water pouring down on us.

I feel more than hear the dark chuckle that dances along the most private part of my body. He pulls back just enough to say, "I might be in love with this bathroom."

I might be in love with you.

But I don't say that. That would defeat the purpose of... of... well, fuck I don't know, his tongue's now *in* my ass, wreaking havoc on my senses. There's really no *might* about it. I'm in love with this guy.

In love with the way he loves me, fiercely and unabashed. The way he makes me feel, the way his mouth feels on my body, *in* my body. *Jesus Christ,* he's *fucking* me with his tongue.

So. Much. *Love.*

All of it. I've got nothing else left in me.

I don't realize I've shut my eyes until I peel them open to look down at where Will's reflection kneels between my legs. From this angle, I can only make out the jut of his jaw as he fucking buries his face between my cheeks. His knees are now digging into the tiled floors, but if his cock is anything to go by—hard and flushed against his stomach, leaving a sticky, glistening mess—he doesn't mind.

A deep-chested groan rises out of me when I feel his stubble scrape over my inner cheeks and thighs, and I don't even care anymore how loud it sounds. The guys could be back and listening in on us for all I fucking care.

He sucks and bites at my rim exactly like he promised me the other day, laving it up with wet, open-mouthed kisses.

"I'm going to devour you. Make you forget everything but the feel of my mouth on you. Gonna make you scream."

To which I told him, *"Bet."*

...knowing full well I'd lose.

My cock stands rigidly against my stomach, balls tingling as he sweeps his tongue over my entrance. Pre-cum weeps from my tip, sliding down the reddened head.

I reach down to give myself a squeeze, some kind of relief, only for Will to pinch my ass. "Hands on the wall."

Nose flaring, teeth gnashing, I do as he says. "Hate you so much."

He stands up suddenly, plastering his front to my back. His dick's hot and hard, wedged between my cheeks. He reaches around with one hand, clasping my jaw, pushing out my lips as he tips my head back.

"No you don't." He presses a kiss to the bridge of my nose, then moves away completely.

"Where the fuck are you going?"

"Need lube."

My ribcage drops with an exhale.

Cold air tingles along my spine and lower. Something wet trails down my inner thigh. *His spit.*

Shudders rack through my body. That shouldn't be as hot as it is.

It feels like an eternity, when really it has to only be seconds before he returns.

The glass slides shut, boxing us in once more. Steam clouds rise above our heads.

"You stayed put," he says, mouth twitching.

I blink at him over my shoulder, muscles tightening as I realize I'm still facing the wall, arms braced against the mirror. Ass out, ready and waiting.

And still, I don't move. What would be the point?

His gaze drifts lazily down my body, teeth sawing into his bottom lip. "I love you like this."

"Just like this?"

A slight shake of his head. "I love you always."

My chest rises. Pretty sure my heart damn near stutters.

His eyes lift to mine, so dark, I can't make out their blues. "But I especially love when you take what you want."

My voice is rough, wrecked as I say, "Pretty sure you'll be doing the taking."

His lips rise. "That so?"

He draws closer, and my gaze drops to the little packet in his hand.

"Came prepared, did you?"

Will grabs my waist with his free hand and presses against my back. His nose is in my wet hair, inhaling deeply. "I'm always prepared."

Pulling back, he lifts the hand not gripping the lube and holds up three fingers in the sign of the Boy Scout salute.

I roll my eyes and grab them, bringing them to my mouth, and snapping my teeth at his fingertips. His shoulders shake with a silent laugh.

He rips the packet of lube open with his teeth.

Damn, that's hot.

Releasing his hand, I turn to face the mirrors once more, bracketing my forearms next to my head.

I watch him through the steam-coated mirror. His hair is wet and slicked back, so I have a perfect view of his down-turned face as he slicks up his fingers with lube. My dick gives a mighty twitch and I bite my lip.

Fuck, ten days is too long to go without this.

And to think a year ago, I actually believed I could go the rest of my *life* without it. Without *this*. Without *him*.

Will steps closer, pressing against me. His other hand comes around front, fingers spreading wide over my clenched stomach.

I spread my legs, giving him easier access as he dips his slicked up fingers down my crease. The lube is chilly and slippery, and I suck in a breath.

"Sorry," he mutters. "Impatient."

I nod jerkily, thinking, *me too.*

His finger skims my hole, gentle, yet prodding.

"Breathe," he whispers, his other hand sliding up to my chest.

I do what he says, releasing the tight hold I have over my muscles, and relax.

Still soft and wet from his mouth and the lube, he has no problem sinking a finger inside me, right down to the knuckle.

My fingers clench over the mirror as I bite down hard on my lip.

"That's it," Will says into a long moan. He drops his mouth to my shoulder as he starts planting open-mouthed kisses over my tingling skin. "Just relax, I got you."

Pressure builds at my hole, awkward and uncomfortable at first as he starts to move in and out, before sneaking in a second finger. I already feel so full, and I'm only going to be fuller.

But I just continue to breathe through it, knowing it will pass. Knowing what comes next. Prepping doesn't take nearly as long as it used to. My body now welcomes the invasion. It's when he leaves that it revolts.

"Goddamn, baby," he says, scissoring two fingers in and out of me. "So fucking tight for me. My balls are aching. Definitely not gonna last once I'm inside you."

A groan scrapes out of me as I tip my head back against his shoulder. He turns his face into my neck, sucking kisses into my flesh, just under my ear. I can feel his chest heaving for air, and we didn't even get to the best part yet.

His deep voice rasps into my ear, "Ready, babe?"

"Uh huh."

I hear his smile in his voice as he says, "Thank God."

His fingers make an obscene squelching sound as he slips them from my hole. I shiver, my shoulders jostling, unable to contain my anticipation.

In the mirror, my mouth dries as I watch Will reach down for the lube packet.

Once he's all slicked up, he tosses what's left back on the ground, grips my waist with his other hand, and pulls me toward him, guiding his cock to my entrance.

He swipes the fat head over my hole, before giving a little nudge to my rim.

A weird little noise escapes me, muffled only slightly by the shower.

"God, I'll never get over the sight of this," he says.

Clenching my fists, I push back, desperate for him to break through that first barrier.

"So fucking hot."

My mouth is so dry, I have to swallow before I can manage to whimper, "Will, please."

I'm fucking dying here, man.

I don't even care that I've been reduced to begging.

In the mirror, I watch as his eyes squeeze shut, his jaw muscles ticking. Like my pleas physically hurt him.

What... But I never get to finish that thought.

The next thing I know, those deep blue eyes are snapping open, blazing into mine just as he reaches up, grips my shoulder, and fucks into me with one powerful thrust.

My mouth opens on a silent gasp as I arch into the glass. Fingers grappling for purchase over the slippery surface. The mirror is wet and ice cold against my bare body. My nipples pebble almost painfully, but I hardly even notice as unbelievable pressure fries my nerve-endings from the inside out.

"Breathe, baby," he chokes out. I can't even be sure *he's* breathing.

He's inside me. *Will's* inside me. Buried so deep within me, it's hard to remember missing him.

He's not moving, just standing there, panting now, with my ass impaled on his cock.

Jesus, did he get bigger since I last saw him?

I almost laugh at the thought, but it turns into a long-winded moan as I throw my head back against his.

"Fuck, I've missed this," he grits out. "Missed you." He grunts, giving the shallowest of thrusts, putting himself impossibly deeper in me. "Missed you so damn much."

The weight of ten long days hangs heavily over each syllable.

"Me too," I barely manage to whisper, tears stinging the back of my eyes. It's all just so fucking *much*.

Something tells me Will hears what I'm not saying, because he suddenly releases my shoulder, seizing my face instead, and guides my mouth to his for a kiss.

It's an awkward angle, so it's more tongue than anything else. Lips sliding messily over our jaws, his rough, mine smooth.

"Love you," I mutter into his chin.

STILL BEATING (PAPERBACK)

Another low grunt punches out of him, and then, without warning, without waiting for my permission, he pulls almost all the way out before slamming back into me.

A grunt bursts out of me as sharp little tingles, like tiny explosions, go off all over my body. It *hurts*, hurts so goddamn good. And I ride that wave of pain and pleasure for as long as it'll carry me.

Don't stop, don't stop, don't stop.

And he doesn't.

He takes me roughly, fucking me without mercy. Without reserve. Just when I think his thrusts will slow into something heady and bone-melting, like they usually do, he changes the angle to assault that white-hot spot inside me. Over and over and *over* again.

Holy fuck.

This time, I *know* the sounds coming out of me are anything but human.

He wins, he wins, he wins all the things, I think stupidly, eyes rolling back into my head.

There's a frantic, almost unhinged edge to the way he's pounding into me, one I've never quite felt from him before. Not like this. It's animalistic and desperate and I realize—

He's been holding back.

The thought forms, settles, then fractures, slipping through my fingers like sand.

That fucker. That beautiful fucking fucker.

Because it doesn't matter. Not what led us here, not what's threatened to tear us apart. The distance we've failed so epically to endure.

Nothing else matters but *this*.

My lips rise of their own volition into a breathless smile. Fingers find their way into my hair, yanking me back. My back arches, pulled tight like a bow.

"Fuck," Will growls through clenched teeth. "I— I can't—"

"D-don't stop," I manage to choke out. I'm nothing more than whimpers and moans as mind-blowing pleasure wrings me out from my head to the tips of my toes. My world starts and ends where we're connected. "D-don't—"

This time, he's the one whimpering. His lips tremble against my neck. "Never."

His hands find mine, linking our fingers together, slamming them to the mirror.

The sound of our wet flesh smacking against each other wars with the water pelting against the tile. With the moans creeping up my throat and Will's short, hard grunts, it's a symphony of all out pleasure. An explosion of the senses.

Nothing else *exists* but this.

Our eyes collide in the steam-streaked mirror, hooded and fierce with love and unbridled wanting.

STILL BEATING (PAPERBACK)

Hunger like nothing I've ever felt before consumes me, and it's a damn crime it took this long to get here. To this moment, where he is me and I am him, and I will *destroy* anything or anybody who tries to sever us.

Unhealthy, my ass. This love is just straight up primal. Our need for each other ingrained in us as deeply as our need for air. Inescapable.

Losing him would literally kill me, and I don't care what anyone has to say about that.

The seconds stretched out between us start to shrink as our pleasure climbs and climbs.

"Will," I whine, clenching his fingers with mine. My cheek's pressed to the mirror. His head is bowed to my neck. I picture him watching us, watching the way our bodies collide.

I'd be jealous if I didn't already feel that collision on an atomic level, every cell of mine igniting as he fucks me so spectacularly.

He groans, driving his cock deep inside me in one smooth glide. This time, he doesn't immediately pull back, just rests against that little bundle of nerves like my entire body isn't trembling around him. Like I'm not about to shatter into a million sparks.

Fuck, fuck, fuck.

"Will, *please.*"

More. I need more. I need—

"Fuck," he bites out, before pulling out of me completely. So fast and sudden, I feel myself gaping from the emptiness. My mouth opens on a gasp, but before I can even process what's happening, he's whirling me around by the waist and dropping to his knees.

Bracing an arm over my middle, he shoves me against the cold, mirrored wall, pinning me.

"Need to taste you," is all he manages to mutter before swallowing my dick down his throat.

Oh my God.

My hands find his hair on instinct, gripping so tight it has to hurt. Has to fucking burn. But if I don't hold onto *something,* I'm going to—

His free hand slides around to palm my ass. Fingers biting into my flesh, squeezing as they creep toward the center. One finds my stretched-out hole, sinking in, down to the root as I clench around the digit.

I'm going to—

Everything's fracturing. Colliding and bursting.

I'm—

He twists his hand, crooks his finger, swallows around my dick with a low, guttural groan that I *feel* and I just—

Explode.

No warning.

No anything.

I'm just—

Gone.

Done.

I'm pretty sure my heart has sunk into my balls. I feel like I'll never stop coming.

My body is quaking, fingers tangled so furiously in his hair, they *hurt*. Will's wild gaze is locked on mine from where he kneels on the shower tile, lips stretched wide around my pulsing cock as he tries to catch every last bit.

When I'm finally spent, I'm dimly aware of him lowering his gaze and carefully easing back off my length. Behind me, his fingers slip out, sliding wetly down the back of my thigh.

I watch through heavily lidded eyes as he lifts a hand to his face and spits all the cum he just collected with his mouth into his palm.

My mouth dries. Pretty sure I'm damn gaping at him, because *holy fuck*.

Still not looking at me, he reaches down and coats his rigid cock in my cum.

My body shudders just as he uses his other hand to grab my waist and buries his face into my thigh, right next to my groin. Inhaling me.

I wanted to do that for him, I think blankly.

I wanted to taste him.

But I'm frozen and tongue-tied, unable to do anything but tug at his hair and squeeze his ears with the heels of my palms. His back muscles quake, shoulders shuddering.

"That's it," I breathe. "Fuck your fist. Soak it with our cum."

His body gives a great jolt at my words, and a beat later, a sharp sting radiates up my side as he bites into my thigh, just under my hip bone. A deep, muffled groan vibrates over my skin as he shatters at my feet.

"Fuck," I mutter, chest collapsing like I've been holding my breath. Maybe I was.

My grip on his skull eases, and I stroke him more gently.

When he starts to pull back, I don't waste a second. I drop down to my knees, clasp his cheeks in my hands and seal our mouths together.

I taste myself on his lips, salty and musky, along with something coppery. *Jesus,* did he break my skin? Draw blood? My lips rise against his at the thought.

Goddamn, City Boy.

He's still trembling, still breathless.

So am I.

Cradling his face, I pull back, searching his eyes with what I'm sure is a goofy, blissed out grin.

His lip is red and swollen. It quivers. "Did I— Did I hurt you?"

STILL BEATING (PAPERBACK)

I shake my head. "Does it look like I'm hurt?"

His eyes pinch at the corners, like he's not sure. It's such a foreign expression to see on his face, especially after sex.

Especially after the best sex I've ever had.

Where's the cocky guy I know and pretend to despise who just fucked me within an inch of my life? He should be damn gloating right now.

"Will," I choke out on a laugh. "Are you serious? That was the single hottest fucking moment of my life. What..." I drift off, blinking fast. I shake my head, unable to find the words. My brain is still offline. I smile stupidly. "How..."

Something softens in his dark blue eyes as they drop to my cheek, before raising once more to my eyes. Some of the worry there easing up as he realizes just how okay I am.

Then it clicks.

"So you have been holding back," I say not unkindly as my earlier suspicion intertwines with what I'm piecing together now.

His lashes flutter over his cheeks as he drops his gaze, confirming as much.

So I smush his cheeks and lift his face, forcing him to meet my steady gaze.

"If you ever hold back with me again," I tell him gravely, fighting a smile. "I'll never forgive you."

Deep ocean blue eyes search mine, like he's looking for something. I don't know what it is, but whatever he finds has redness creeping around the edges and tears welling at the bottoms.

What the—

My grip on his face loosens just as he chokes out, "I-I missed you."

My shoulders drop. Chest collapses. Heart splits wide open.

This guy. This fucking guy.

Will hangs his head, and I don't think, I just wrap him in my arms, and pull him close to me. Tucking his face into my shoulder as I hug him as hard as I can.

"I missed you so much," he says into my neck, his voice thick and muffled as strong arms come around me. Water continues to cascade down on us, still hot somehow, though we've long since gotten used to it.

Eyes burning, throat tight, I nod against his head. "I know, baby. I know."

He shudders and I squeeze my eyes shut.

Our exhaustion is this living, breathing thing between us. I can feel his as much as mine. And while there's relief there too, I can't help but acknowledge the dread creeping its spindly unwanted fingers around our shoulders. Whispering into our ears as we hold ourselves tighter, breathe in each other harder.

As if we could push away the inevitable with the sheer force of our will and love alone.

My mouth twitches sadly at the thought. *Pun intended.*

"I'm sorry."

"Shut up," I tell him, voice breaking. I bury my nose in his wet hair. "Shut up so hard."

His shoulders shake at that and I smile.

He's bigger than me, only just. And usually a force strong enough to withstand anything.

But tonight, right now, he's mine to hold. Mine to protect. Mine to shield from what tomorrow might bring.

It took fucking forever for him to let me see him like this. To let me *in*. Months spent trying to be stoic and fierce as he helped me fight off *my* demons...

Only for the demons at his back to gather an army and pull him under when we least expected it. When he could no longer hold them back alone and I was left grappling.

I squeeze my eyes shut until I see spots.

We weren't good for each other last year.

I wasn't good for *him*.

Because he was in Hell too, and I was too weak to see it. Too weak to do much of anything but hang on for dear life to whatever I could grab.

He's still there sometimes, as am I.

But I'm stronger now.

Strong enough to withstand whatever comes *his* way... even if I can't always be strong enough for myself.

Pun 110 percent intended.

Because that's why I have him, I remind myself.

To always have my back. To always catch me when I fall.

Just as I'll have his. Just as I'll catch him.

And if we fall together, then so be it. Our strength goes beyond just the two of us. That's what family's for. That's what we have thorns for. Tethering us even when things get ugly.

"We're gonna be okay," I promise him, smiling into his hair.

Fingers dig into my back, clutching onto me. "Still beating?" Will rasps, just loud enough for me to hear.

I blow out a breath, tip my head back toward the Heavens, and squint into the downpour of water just like I did earlier in the rain.

"Yeah," I tell him strongly. "Still beating."

6

WILL FOSTER

AT FIRST I'M NOT sure what woke me.

I blink heavily against the sleep still clinging to my aware-ness, momentarily confused when the room around me sharpens into focus.

It's dark, so it must still be nighttime, but the cracked open door sheds just enough light in the room for me to make out my surroundings.

That's not my ceiling.

"Shit, sorry," a voice whispers, barely audible over the steady hum of the fan coming from the unit under the window. Footsteps sound over the floor, muffled against the carpet. I think I hear something like paper rustling.

Frowning, I pinch the corners of my eyes, and roll my head to the side to take in the hooded, hunched figure creeping across the room.

The hell?

I'm on my back, which isn't how I usually sleep, telling me just how fucking exhausted I am. A warm, heavy weight is plastered against my right side. An inked arm is thrown over my chest. Soft puffs of air blow on my bare chest where Waylon's face is smushed against my pec.

"We brought food back with us. Wasn't sure if you'd still be awake, but..." The voice I now recognize as Mason's trails off as the guy passed out on top of me grumbles something in his sleep. "I'll just leave the bag here."

My mouth crooks up and I nod. "Thanks."

A beat passes, like he's hesitating. Just when I'm sure he's gonna forget it and leave, he speaks.

"I know you're worried," he whispers in a rush. "I know it's hard. But we've got him, okay? We won't let anything happen. He had a bad day. We all do. But we get through them."

My throat tightens with emotion as I remember what happened outside the hotel.

"This wasn't part of the plan," Waylon had said, and all I can think now is, *no shit.* Our reunion should've been a happy one. Not... that.

But I try not to think about that right now. I'm too fucking tired. And even though I haven't eaten in over twenty-four hours, I can't find it in me to even care right now.

"I know," I say quietly.

"Do you?"

My mouth parts but closes at that. *Do I?*

Another long moment passes, before he says more gently, "It'll get easier. With time. It took Phoebe months before she could look at me without breaking down in sobs after I ODed." He pauses. "Taking even longer for Jer to forgive me for last year."

I still at that, blinking hard into the thin darkness.

Does he know I know?

I doubt that. As far as I'm aware, they're still not talking. Not while Jeremy's abroad for school. He wanted space to get over Mason, and Mason's giving it to him.

"He'll come around," I finally manage to say.

A beat passes. "Maybe."

My brows crash down over my eyes. He sounds... odd. Closed off, and something else I can't pinpoint.

"I wouldn't blame him if he didn't. I—" He mumbles something I can't make out. "Never mind, this isn't about me."

My confusion only grows. God, I'm way too tired for this conversation.

"Anyway, I just... wanted to make sure you guys got food. He hasn't eaten since breakfast, and—" He blows out a breath. "I doubt you ate anything either. So, take care of yourselves, okay?" He swallows with a loud click into the quiet room. "We need you. Both of you."

An ache forms in my chest and I nod, taking care not to jostle Waylon's sleeping form. "Thanks, man. I mean it. For..." I suck in a breath and release it slowly. "Thanks for being there for him when I can't be. Shawn too."

"Always."

His footsteps move farther away, heading toward the door. I bite my lip, debating...

Just as the door creaks open, allowing him enough room to slip through, I whisper out his name.

Fuck it.

He pauses with his back to me.

"He's okay, you know," I say, wondering if it'd be better to just shut my trap. I don't clarify who I'm referring to. "Happy, last I talked to him. Said he met someone."

All true.

It's impossible to tell for sure, but I swear Mason stiffens the faintest bit.

"Good," he says after a moment, voice stilted. "That's good."

And with that he leaves, closing the door behind him. Darkness envelops the room once more, utterly black at first until my eyes adjust.

If they're just getting back now with food, we must've not been asleep for long. Pretty sure I was out as soon as my head hit the pillow. I only vaguely remember sluggishly drying off and creeping back to Waylon's room, our fingers and toes pruned from how long we sat huddled together in the shower.

And here I thought I was the one coming to the rescue.

I huff a humorless laugh at that and turn my head, burying my nose in his still-damp hair.

How is it that he's right here, and I already miss him?

His arm twitches, and then he mumbles something, before rolling over onto his other side, away from me. He's definitely unconscious, and yet he scoots back, snuggling into me.

My lips rise as I follow his lead and roll onto my side, sliding my arm over his waist. I take my other arm, which is numb and tingly from him lying on it, and shove it under the pillow under his head.

We're both bare ass naked under the covers, having opted out of getting dressed once we shut ourselves back in here for the night. My soft cock presses against his ass as I cuddle close, spooning him.

Nose pressed to his nape, I inhale.

He's really here.

No... *I'm* really here. In LA. On the other side of the fucking country. God, has it really only been twenty-four hours since I got that phone call?

Waylon stirs slightly, mumbling something before smacking his lips. Then his breathing evens out once more, telling me he's still fast asleep.

He's always been such a light sleeper, so it's weird to have the roles reversed. Kind of nice actually, seeing as I rarely get to witness something as simple as Waylon sleeping peacefully. Feeling him relaxed and boneless in my arms.

Normally, he's either waking up at the ass crack of dawn, hours before me, ready to start his day with a jog. Or he's gasping awake from nightmares he can't remember, muscles rigid, fingers clenched in my arms.

Or he's waking *me* up from nightmares I remember all too well. Shaking me, lips pressed together in a tight, bloodless line, eyes creased with worry as all I can do is stare at him, not sure if my mind's playing tricks on me.

The world grows heavy once more as sleep beckons me back. My thoughts splintering into nonsense.

I like this, I think. Not even sure what I like, but it has the ache that's been in my chest for days finally easing up, breaking off into something softer. Easier to withstand.

My hand slides up Waylon's bare chest.

His heart pounds and pounds and pounds, a steady rhythm I'm well familiar with.

"It gets easier," Mason said.

And as I lay here, cuddled with the boy I love, his heart beating sturdily against my palm as sleep drags me under once more...

I can believe it does.

⚹

THIS TIME, IT'S THE quiet strum of guitar strings that wakes me. Gently, like finger-strokes over my hair. Or a breeze fluttering in through the window.

And still I bury my face into the pillow and groan.

"Morning, Sunshine."

I reach up and flip him off.

He chuckles.

Okay, so I'm not a morning person. Never claimed to be. It just didn't take until we were dating and practically living together for him to figure out just how much of a bear I am in the morning, especially before coffee.

He loves to give me shit for it. For such a grump, he's quite infuriatingly chipper in the mornings. It's like he sucks all the happy out of me while I sleep, converting it into energy.

Fucking incubus.

Music continues to fill the room, slightly louder now that he knows I'm awake.

I don't recognize the song, so either it's a new one they've been working on, or it's new period. It wouldn't be the first time I woke up to Waylon playing around with something. It would seem early mornings, or coming right out of a heavy sleep, are when inspiration strikes hardest.

There's also the fact the sheet is bunched at the bottom of the bed, leaving my naked ass bare to the world. I'm not conceited enough to think he's waxing poetic about my body right now, but also, I am that conceited. I have a good body, a muse-worthy ass even, perhaps—I work hard in the gym for it—and I have it on good authority he loves it.

I just might love *his* a little bit more. I just prefer to fuck him senseless than try to spin sonnets about it. *Talented fucker,* I grouse inwardly without any heat. He's got more musical talent in his pinkie nail than I've got in my entire body.

Yawning into my arm, I finally roll over and push up into a seated position. Running my hands through my hair, I wince when I hit a couple snags. It's gotta look wild from going to sleep with it wet.

A quick glance at Waylon shows his hair is all curly and tousled too.

"What?" he says, looking at me through hooded eyes. He's still shirtless, but he threw on a pair of gray sweatpants. *Pity.*

Teeth gnawing into my bottom lip, I shake my head.

"The guys dropped off food while we were sleeping," he eventually says, fingers stilling on his guitar. He jerks his head toward the bag rumpled up at the bottom of the bed. "I ate mine already. Sorry. But I got you coffee from the lobby."

Scratching my jaw, I reach for the to-go cup he gestures to on the nightstand.

"It's probably cold by now," he tries to warn me softly, but I'm already guzzling it down.

"Don't care," I rasp, wiping the back of my hand across my mouth. Blinking a couple times, I screw my eye shut against the orange sunlight streaming in through a gap in the curtains. "What time is it?"

"A little after one."

I whip my head at him, eyes bugging out. "In the afternoon?"

He smiles and nods. "Yeah."

"Shit, I'm sorry," I start saying, rubbing my chest, but he's already shaking his head.

"I slept so hard the first day here. Jet lag's a bitch, and I've been told it'll be even worse when we get home."

My knuckles pause as everything in me stills.

He seems to realize too what he just said, and everything that happened yesterday rushes back to the forefront, hanging heavily between us.

Because the fact of the matter is simple, sitting in me like an unmovable stone.

We won't be going home together.

I swallow hard, and dig my nails into the cup.

"Will..."

"Are you okay?" I ask, lifting my gaze up at him through my lashes.

His eyes tighten. "Shouldn't I be asking you that?"

I shake my head. "I meant... Are you sore?"

He rolls his eyes, but I don't miss the slight flush on his cheeks. "I'm fine. I'm sitting, aren't I?"

A low creaky chuckle escapes me at that.

"It's a good hurt, Will," he assures me quietly. Something in his voice has me sobering. He smiles, and it's a gentle smile, almost wistful. "Really good."

Jesus.

"Masochist," I mutter taking another sip of cold coffee.

His grin widens, dark brows wagging. "Sadist."

STILL BEATING (PAPERBACK)

My gaze drops to the dimples sinking deeply in his cheeks, and my chest tightens. Mouth dries. Coffee goes down like ash.

I set the cup back down on the table.

"Will—"

"You were happy," I hear myself say, my voice no louder than a whisper.

"What?" he whispers back. Not moving his furrowed gaze off my face, he reaches down to set the guitar on the floor, before scooting closer to me and grabbing my lifeless hands.

I drop my attention to our laced fingers, finally tighten them around his. "Last night. When you got to the hotel. You were happy." I force a hard swallow and finally look up to meet his wary hazel eyes. "You were smiling and laughing and singing and…"

My voice trails off. I don't need to finish the thought, but he finishes it for me anyway.

"You thought I was drunk."

My face bunches and I look away.

"Hey."

His hands squeeze mine, jostling me a bit to get my attention.

I drop my gaze before dragging it back up to his.

"I'm not mad," he says.

"You were."

"Yeah, for a second," Waylon admits. "But I get it. I didn't at first, but... I get it. It makes sense why you thought that, especially given what happened the other night."

I study him, not sure I believe him. Not sure I can even come up with the words to explain what was going on in my head at that moment. Hell, not just that moment, but that entire day. It's like as soon as I got on that plane and had no choice but to sit there, without any way of him getting in touch with me or me getting in touch with him, I just...

Lost it.

"Maybe..." he starts hesitantly. He tries again. "Maybe next time I... have an episode, they don't call you."

I stare blankly at him.

His throat works with a swallow, and I can visibly see the struggle in his hazel eyes. The flicker of fear at not being able to come to me when he needs me. It's a fear as familiar to me as my own.

"I don't like that plan."

His brows lift. "Neither do I, but the alternative is..."

"Me coming to LA," I say flatly.

He was happy. He was happy and I ruined it.

He makes a face. "What? You have to know I'm... God, happy doesn't even begin to cover it. You being here..." Shaking his head, he looks down, blowing out a harsh breath.

I don't say anything at first. I just wait, tense and unsure, because I want to believe him. And today, in the light of day, after the first restful sleep I've had in over a week, I feel like I *could* believe him. I just...

"I don't want to make anything worse for you." The words tumble from my lips stilted and unbidden.

His head snaps up at that.

I vaguely remember saying or asking something similar last night. And yet, the admission tastes even more sour on my tongue the second time around. But it's too late to take it back, even if I could. It's out there now.

"Will," he says, slowly shaking his head. "I... Are you serious right now?" he says, voice cracking. Releasing one of his hands from mine, he brings it up to rub roughly down his face. "Do you know what you didn't see last night, before all the singing and laughing?" Not waiting for me to respond, he drops his hand to his lap and says, "Me losing my shit on the streets of LA all because I was dreading going back to an empty bed."

It takes a second for his words to process, but when they do, I swear my heart grinds to a stop.

His face pinches and he looks almost angry as he throws a careless hand out, gesturing at nothing. "I was a fucking mess and I couldn't even admit to the guys why. They knew, of course they fucking knew. But I couldn't tell them how much I was missing you, because it felt *weak*. Needing you felt fucking weak. It was easier to admit to them I wanted a drink."

My lashes flutter closed at that. "Babe—"

"And I did. I *wanted* a drink. I wanted to drink 'til I passed out. I wanted to drink until Saturday arrived, and you were here, and I could hold you and not feel like I'm breaking apart inside."

I'm not sure whose fingers are squeezing whose anymore.

My eyes open, no doubt red-rimmed as they clash with his glistening gaze.

"You showing up like that..." he says, shaking his head.

"It wasn't part of the plan," I say, repeating his words from last night.

He throws his hand out again. "I said that because I thought it was my fault." Compressing his fingers into a fist, Waylon presses it to the center of his chest. "I thought you dropped everything and flew here because I had a stupid panic attack. I was mad at myself, Will, not at you for showing up. I just— I wanted to be strong enough. I wanted to make it to Saturday, for *me.*"

"And I ruined that."

He groans. "Jesus fucking Christ, shut up. *Shut up!*"

I blink wide at his outburst.

"You're not listening, or maybe I'm just not saying this right." He huffs and runs his fingers through his messy dark hair. "I said *was*. Past-tense. All past-tense. I don't... I was just being stubborn. And selfish. And-and..."

"Way," I breathe.

"I don't know how to talk about this without making it about me, and I'm sick of making it about me. Because it's not. It's about you too. It's—"

"Hey," I say, scooting closer, ducking my head to find his gaze. "Stop. I know."

He sniffs, staring into me with such sadness it steals my breath. "I hate feeling like I failed you."

My brow knits. "What? Where did that come from? How the fuck did you fail me?"

"If I was strong enough, if I didn't... panic over a stupid fucking frying pan..." He shakes his head. "You'd've had no reason to move up your flight. I know... I know me falling apart is a trigger for you. I get that. Maybe now more than ever. Which is why I just—"

I release his hands and hurriedly cup his cheeks, jerking his gaze to mine. "Do you really think that's the only reason I'm here? That that's the only reason I fell apart last night?"

His features tighten, eyes darkening with some unnamed emotion.

"You heard me," I say slowly, voice raw and strung tight, "when I told you I missed you. Right?"

Tears well in his eyes but don't fall. He nods jerkily.

I inhale deeply, before releasing it. "What you don't know is that I went to the airport twice in the last week before actually stepping foot inside the doors. Confirmed a change in flights *twice* before actually sticking to one and getting on the fucking plane."

Huffing out a sharp, humorless laugh, I look away. "Ivy knew it was coming. She all but threatened me, or rather, threatened *you,* to get me on the plane this time. Not that I needed it." I pause as my gaze grows far-off and unfocused. "There's no telling if I would've made it to Saturday, even if I didn't get that call. I was almost," —I scrunch up my face— "*grateful,*" I spit. "Grateful you were freaking out so I had an excuse to come out here."

When he doesn't immediately say anything, I turn to look at him.

His eyes are wide and so very, very gold in the orange afternoon light.

"And then, I got here, and you weren't at the hotel. My phone was dead. The man at the desk said you might be at a bar—"

He's rapidly shaking his head.

"—so I waited. I waited and imagined the worst. So when I saw you turn the corner..." My voice breaks off and I shake my head.

"You saw I was happy and thought the only way I could be happy was if I was drunk."

I squeeze my eyes shut. "Because if you were happy sober, then why the fuck would you need me here?"

Arms come around me as he all but tackles me back against the headboard.

"Will." He squeezes me. "You're such an idiot."

I choke out a sound that is equal part laugh, equal part sob.

He pulls back, gripping my shoulders. His hazel eyes are bright with unshed tears, but he's smiling. "You stupid, stupid idiot."

"That's not very nice," I say quietly, lip twitching.

Eyes still wide on mine, he says, "And here I've been freaking out, thinking you only need *me* when *I'm* falling apart."

I blink at him.

He swallows with a loud click. "That you only miss me when... when you're scared for me, or-or... feel like you need to fix something, fix *me*."

I curl my lip up at that. "What? I told you you're not a fucking project to me."

Smiling sadly, he shakes his head. Dimples peeking out, slowly, then more deeply. "I know. I know that. Doesn't mean

I don't... worry." He shrugs. "The whole foundation of our relationship rests on fucking trauma, man. You gotta wonder sometimes. Who are we without it? Not just us individually, but as a couple."

Another blink.

Is he fucking serious?

"I mean," he goes on gently, "you just said it yourself." He gestures at my chest with his inked fingers. "If I was happy sober, why would I still need you?"

I—

My head thumps back against the headboard. "Shit."

I feel more than see his shoulders deflate as I stare unseeingly up at the white ceiling.

He's right to be worried, isn't he?

My breakdown last night makes a little more sense now.

"No," I say quickly. Then louder, more determined, "Nope, no, fuck that."

I sit up and reach for him. His cheeks are only slightly rougher than they were last night in the shower. His jaw works in the cradle of my palms as I stare into those gorgeous, glistening hazel eyes of his.

"If you think I only want you when you're..." Lifting my shoulders, I look around aimlessly for the right words, as if they're buried somewhere in these hotel walls. "At your worst then.... then, *fuck,* I'm sorry. 'Cause that just means I haven't been doing a good enough job to prove to you that's not the case."

"Will, no—" he starts to protest.

"Shush," I say, pressing my thumb over his lips. He glares at me, bringing a small grin to my face as I say, "It's okay. It... helps knowing that that's something that's been bothering you."

He shakes his head, tries to say something, but I only add pressure to his lips, until his teeth dig into my skin.

"Even if you didn't realize it 'til now," I amend gently, reassuring him. I know this is not something he's consciously worried about. On good days, it's easy to see how we work. Easy to see how much we love each other, no matter what.

But on the bad days... Days like yesterday...

Days where we're miles and miles away from one another, with only the bad memories to keep us company in the dark...

It's easy to forget.

Easy for our worst fears to slip in behind us unawares.

His throat bobs with a swallow. Lifting a hand, he pries my thumb off his mouth so he can speak. "If that's the case, then that means I haven't been doing a good enough job to prove to you that for as much as I need and rely on you, I want you and love you ten times more."

I roll my lips together at that and shake my head. I don't want to believe that. I *don't*. I know he loves me. Wants me.

He shows it all the time. In every touch, every kiss. This cold ass coffee he got for me, made just like I like it.

He arches a brow, eyes remaining steady on mine. "Or we're both just really fucking stubborn."

Barking out a laugh, I tip my head. "Or that."

His mouth crooks up, dimple sinking in his cheek.

I stroke my thumb over it. "One day."

"One day?"

Leaning forward, I feather a kiss against his lips. He exhales against my mouth, tasting of mint, coffee, and something sweet that's all him.

Bowing my head to his, I stare deep into his eyes, giving him no choice but to see me. Hear me as I vow, "One day, I'm going to get it through your thick, stubborn skull that you matter."

He stills.

"Not just to me, but especially to me." I swallow tightly. "That you don't just..." —I wet my lips, searching his bright eyes— "disappear when no one's looking."

Something breaks in his gaze at that, telling me I hit the nail on the head.

It's been a while since I so viciously wanted to bring Seamus McAllister back from the dead, just so I can break him apart piece by piece. Give him a taste of what he did to his son. His own flesh and blood.

STILL BEATING (PAPERBACK)

My jaw clenches as I keep my hand gentle on his cheek. A part of me will always be gentle with him, no matter how much he might want otherwise. Sure, fucking him rough is one thing, but this... moments like these...

It's the fact that I know he would prefer abrasiveness that keeps my touch soft.

"You don't just stop existing when we're not together," I tell him. Grabbing his hand, I bring it to my chest. "You exist in here." I push his knuckles against where my heart thumps strongly, ensuring he can feel it. "So long as this thing keeps beating, you're not going anywhere. On the good days, the bad days, and everything in between. Even when you're miles and miles away from me."

His jaw quivers in my hand.

Wetting my lips again, I rock my head against his. "I might love you harder when you're at your worst, but that's only because you need it harder then. But my love for you when you're at your best?" I release a breath, smiling. "It's unmatched. It consumes me."

Pulling back, I tip his head back, cradling it in my palms.

His eyes are hooded and so, so soft on mine.

I smile down at him. "What happened last night was all on me. My fears. If I could've seen beyond them, I would've realized how... relieved I was. Proud, even." I shrug. "Last winter, panic attacks took you out for days sometimes. And the fact you let the guys be there for you..." I shake my head, emotion clogging my throat as I finish thickly, "Shows just how far you've come."

Against my palms, I feel his throat work with a swallow.

"You got through it without me." I nod. "That's a good thing. Really good."

His nose flares. "It doesn't mean I need you any less."

I start to smile, but he keeps going, voice rough with determination to prove himself to me. Prove his love for me.

"That I don't want you just as fiercely as I always do. Hell, the whole time we were walking back to the hotel, I couldn't wait to call you and tell you that I-I was okay. I missed you, so fucking much, and sleeping alone..." He shakes his head. "It was gonna be a bad night, but I..." He lifts his shoulders and drops them. "More than that, I just hated that I was enjoying myself, even for a moment, without you by my side."

My heart stutters at that.

He reaches up, clasping my neck in his hands as he crushes our foreheads together once more. Our noses smush, but he doesn't make any move to fix that.

Staring deep into my eyes, he says, "One day, *I'm* going to get it through *your* thick, stubborn skull that I love you even more when I'm happy."

My entire being seems to just clench and release as Waylon's words sink in. Pulling apart some of the tension I didn't even realize was there, and setting it free.

"That for as much as I need you when shit's all dark and fucked up in my head, I love you just as much, if not more so, when I'm clear-headed. When I feel strong and capable, and not strangled by the fear that I'm going to lose you, or by the voices that try to convince me you deserve better."

"Way..."

He inhales deeply, bringing us impossibly closer. "My love for you when I'm sad and scared is very selfish. Even a little ugly. But when I'm happy, it's pure. Easy and simple as breathing."

I squeeze my eyes shut. "Is it wrong that I want it all? The ugly and the pure. I'll take it all."

He chuckles against my mouth. "Greedy."

"When it comes to you, yeah."

I feel his smile against my lips. "Of course it's all yours," he whispers. "For as long as you want it, it's yours."

"Always," I say automatically.

He laughs outright this time, the vibrations tickling my lips. "Not even gonna think about it?"

"No."

He makes a noise in the back of his throat, then a hand comes around my nape, squeezing. "You're ridiculous."

I don't try to deny it. Instead, I kiss him.

Our mouths explore each other slowly and heavily, like we have all day. Like we don't need to part for air. It's a searing kiss, the kind that stokes the flames, building and building until I know we'll eventually, inevitably, combust from the pressure.

All I can do is hope that once it settles, enough embers will have reached those dark, cold, deserted places where loneliness lives and fear thrives.

Fuck if I don't ever want this fire to die.

"How long do we have?" he whispers, as if sensing where my thoughts have gone. His lips slide over my jaw, teeth scraping my stubble.

I shiver, throwing my head back to give him better access. "Five days."

"Two more than planned, then."

Smiling, I hold his face to my neck. His tongue lashes out against my overheated skin, and I thrust up against him, bringing out a low, raspy chuckle just over my racing pulse.

"After that?" I manage to whisper, knowing it needs to be addressed.

Lifting his head, he smiles up at me with that peaceful, dimpled grin. Eyes like sunlit forests stare back at me. "After that, we try again."

Pushing away some of the dark messy hair from his eyes, I nod. "We try again."

Knowing it's our only option. Knowing it's what's best, no matter how much we now know it'll hurt.

It will get easier.

I have to believe that.

His lips find mine once more, and my hands are down his sweats, smoothing over his warm skin. We're bare chest to bare chest, hearts racing wildly as we lose ourselves once more to this messy, stubborn love of ours.

Maybe we failed this time.

Maybe we'll keep failing.

Maybe that's the point.

7

WAYLON MCALLISTER

TONIGHT'S GONNA BE A good night.

Mason and I finish belting out the final chorus to our newest—and *improved*—track, "Sun Chaser," headphones cupped tightly over our ears, neck tendons straining as we lean up against our respective mics.

With our hooded, heated gazes locked on one another's, it's as if we're silently daring each other not to stop. As if we're silently spurring each other on. *Come on, come on. Higher, higher.*

We've already hit that pivotal pitch where our voices merged into one seamless, harmonized sound, so why not see how far we can take it?

Why not see what we're capable of *together?*

Maybe some musicians would resent it, but I'm not one of them. And neither is Mason. This is about connecting, not competing. And all I can think is, *this. This is what was missing.*

For days, this song has been the bane of my existence, despite how good it felt when I first wrote it on the plane. A six-hour fevered rush where nothing else existed but the lyrics pouring out of my pen, and the melody playing in my head.

As soon as we landed in LA and got settled in the hotel, I unpacked my guitar and let the song trapped in my chest finally breathe. And it felt *good,* so damn good. Like a soft gust of fresh air, rather than teeth-squeezing anguish, like the majority of the songs I wrote or co-wrote.

It felt *easy.* Like it was meant to be. And I didn't mind sharing it with Paul, our agent, or even the label once he decided, *Yes, yes, this is the* one! and all but dragged our tired asses to the studio.

I was all about adding it to the album, still running on that high of finishing something. Hell, I was *itching* to share it with everyone, the entire world if I could.

But then the label started doing that thing labels do. Somehow, this one single song set off a chain of events as it became a sort of anchoring counterpoint to the whole album.

Suddenly, it's to be our first official single under Slater Records.

Suddenly, it's the name of our debut album.

Suddenly, this is what our whole fucking *brand* is going to be based on.

And I just... I felt sick. I hated it. Hated what it had become. Something that was supposed to be softer and personal—something to be woven into the darker chapters of our lives to shine a little bit of light and give a little bit of hope—was standing front and center, potentially overshadowing everything else.

It felt like a lie. Like a disservice to everything we've been through—what we're all *still* going through—all the blood, sweat, and tears poured into an album that's been years in the making.

It no longer felt like *us.*

And fuck if I was scared people would no longer appreciate all the rest, if this is what the Lost Boys ended up being known for outside of the bubble of TikTok.

Our grief—our pain—is *loud,* maybe even too loud to be digestible. So I get it. I get why the label has every reason to want to market the album around this one lighter song, especially with it being our first.

To them, it's just business. It's all about the money, about what sells, what's marketable.

But for us, music is what saved our lives. What *keeps* on saving our lives.

It's what kept our hearts beating when it felt like we had nothing else. It's every vice of ours, every demon, channeled into something a little less ugly. Something that feels... *purposeful.*

And that's not something I, or the guys, are willing to sacrifice, even if it means we don't reach as many people as we would if we just "lighten up a bit."

Not Paul's exact words, but that's the gist of it. And I know he wasn't trying to be a dick about it. He just doesn't get it. He wasn't there. He's never been on our side of the fence.

He's one of the lucky ones, I suppose, and that's *okay.* That just means we have to push a little harder to stay true to ourselves.

My thoughts return to the present just as Mason and I let the last note fade as one.

He's nodding, and so am I. Both of our chests heaving, like we're still connected in some indefinable way.

I wet my lips, slide the headphones off, and glance toward the glass where Bryce, our producer, and Paul give up enthusiastic thumbs up.

"That was it," Mason whispers.

Sliding him a sideways glance, my mouth crooks up as I pant, "Yeah."

That was it.

Don't get me wrong. I *love* the original, lighter version of this song and what it stood for. Not only my song for *Will,* but my song for me, for what kept me hanging on when literally nothing else did, music and my family included.

But I only love it as much as I do because *I* was the one who *lived* it. I lived the darkness that led up to that perfect sunrise. I appreciate it in a way I don't think many others could.

And it's that fucking fact that made me ultimately decide the world's not ready for it. *I'm* not ready for the world to have it.

It's still there, though, that underlying heartbeat. But it's no longer so glaring compared to the rest of the album. The song is grittier now. It's edgy and raw. Something worthy of being the title track without sacrificing who we are at our core.

At least, who we are *now.*

Maybe the original will fit one day, but we're not there yet. *I'm* not there yet.

This is just our beginning. And I'm not about to rush through all the dark, ugly stuff, just to make it more palatable to those on the outside looking in.

Outside the sound booth, Bryce meets us with hand slaps. "That was the one! You fuckin' killed it."

Shawn appears behind him, nodding.

I swallow and nod back before risking a glance at Paul. Despite the thumbs up he gave us, I can't help but worry he'll still insist we need to add something lighter, more cheery.

His head's cocked as he studies me. Not Mason, but *me,* and I try not to squirm.

Paul knew what he got into when we hired him, and hell, it's even written somewhere in our contract. Not just with him, but the label. We do this, but we do it our way. That was always the deal.

We made it clear from the fucking start that just because we're from a small town and don't come from money, that we're not willing to sell our souls to this industry. And if they couldn't accept that from the get-go—if they weren't willing to meet us halfway, despite how risky it could be for them financially—then we walk. Simple as that.

Either we'd find someone else to back us, or we'd go indie. It didn't really matter to us, so long as we got to keep making music.

"If you ever want to strip that song down and do an acoustic version, let me know," is all he eventually says. There's a look in his eye I can't really place. He glances down. "It's too personal as it was. I get that now."

My brow furrows. *Does he though? What changed?*

But then my eyes catch on the guy still seated across the room, blue eyes twinkling my way, and I realize, *Oh.*

Maybe that's what changed.

Scrubbing his jaw, Paul looks away. "You're not the first sad saps I've worked with, believe it or not." He chuckles quietly, almost tiredly. "But it's my job to try and push you, okay?" He turns to face me once more, brown eyes more serious than I've ever seen them. "To see who you are outside your comfort zone, whatever that is."

My throat dries at what he's saying, what he's implying.

Next to me, Mason shifts, brushing my shoulder with his, telling me he's drawing the same conclusions.

Paul smiles. "You call the shots. The three of you. That never changes." He pauses, glancing at each of us, Shawn included, who has now joined our side. "I never wanted to be a sell-out either, and I'd like to think I've been successful so far. My loyalty is to you, never the label. Okay?"

I nod, and in my periphery, Mason and Shawn do the same.

He bounces his gaze between the three of us. "I could tell something was off, but I knew you needed to figure it out yourselves, figure out what *you* wanted, and see outside the expectations of everyone around you."

Bryce gives a firm nod, backing Paul's words up.

"As much as I—*we* appreciate you trying to appease the powers that be..." he trails off, shaking his head. "It's not necessary. But..." Again he trails off, but this time a smile crawls its way up his cheek. "I'm really fucking happy with what came out of it. So maybe a little pressure is good, yeah?"

Mason chuckles as I roll my eyes.

"Yeah," I tell him. "It's good."

He claps his hands together, rubbing them. Turning to say something to Bryce, he waves Mason over to the deck to have a listen. He probably means for me too, but that can wait.

This can't.

Will sits sprawled on the red leather couch on the opposite side of the room, arms stretched over the back. Legs spread. His head cocks when he sees me striding toward him, dark wavy blonde hair curling over his eye.

Fuck, my boyfriend's hot.

"Hey there, Cupcake," he says easily, his voice deep in that naturally smoky timber of his.

For half a second, I consider just plopping down on his lap. But we're far from alone right now, and I'm not *that* comfortable with PDA yet. Especially of the lap-sitting variety. Probably never will be.

So instead, I settle for plopping down next to him, throwing a leg over his. Resting my arm just next to his on the back of the couch, I search his face as I ask, "How was it?"

His mouth ticks up as he tilts his head side to side in a so-so gesture. "I mean, I'm a little biased."

"Only a little?"

His grin widens. "It was fucking perfect."

I suck in my cheeks, holding back a smile of my own.

"I mean," he says, "don't get me wrong, I'm definitely *way* more biased when it comes to the original."

Rolling my eyes, I huff a short laugh through my nose, remembering how I played it for him and only him last night.

After we finally managed to pry ourselves away from the bed yesterday, we met up with the guys for a late dinner once they were done in the studio, and got Will all caught up on what's been going on. Or rather, what's *not* been going on.

"It just doesn't feel right," I had told him. *"Something's off."*

Then I went on to explain that it wasn't even just that I was miserable without him. It went deeper than that, but I just couldn't put my finger on it. The guys were in agreement. While missing the shit out of Will definitely put me in a funk, there was more to the block than just that.

It was confirmed when we got back to the hotel, and we secluded ourselves in my room, and I took out my guitar and played the song I wrote for him. Will. My guy. Sunshine personified, even on the gloomy days.

God, that look on his face...

I'll write him a song a day for the rest of our lives if it means getting to see that look on his face again.

But it was after playing it for Will that I realized what was off about it all.

It wasn't the *song* that was the problem. It was sharing it with anyone other than Will that felt gross. Wrong.

"It's easier," I hear myself say as I return to the present, "to be sad."

Will's brow knits. "What do you mean?"

Gulping, I look up at him through my lashes. "People shit on happy things all the time."

"They shit on sad things too," he says slowly, eyeing me carefully.

"But it's... easier..."

Understanding lights up his blue eyes, widening them.

Behind me, I hear Mason's and my voices playing back through the speakers, isolated from any instrument. So perfectly harmonized, it sends a chill down my spine hearing it.

"You're protective of it," Will says quietly, nodding, as if confirming something to himself. "The happy stuff. The good stuff." *Us,* I hear, even if he doesn't say it out loud.

Pressing my lips together tightly, I simply nod back.

What Paul just said before, about pushing us out of our comfort zone... combined with what Will told me yesterday...

"You don't just disappear when no one's looking."

...It all finally clicked. The reason why this has been so hard. I'm... fuck, I'm *comfortable* being miserable. Not only that, but I'm comfortable talking about it too. Between therapy and meetings and just all the shit I've had to deal with over the last year—hell, my whole life—I've gotten used to baring all the ugly to the world, scars and flaws and all.

Because it served a purpose.

It felt meaningful.

What I'm not used to is sharing... this. The moments no one else gets to see. The moments where I am happy for literally no other reason than I get to turn to Will and ask him something as trivial as what he wants to eat for dinner tonight.

Moments, like now, where I reach for his hand like it's nothing, and not because I'm choking on panic, chest blazing with the need to breathe.

"I don't want anyone to ruin this," I whisper, loosely tangling our fingers together where they rest over the back of the couch.

His other hand finds my chin, lifting my head until I'm eye-level with those deep ocean blues.

"No one can ruin this."

"But they can try."

He scowls. "So? Let 'em. I dare them to."

A quiet laugh slips through my lips. He makes it sound so easy.

"You're scared," he says. There's a finality to his tone that leaves no room for argument. "I get that."

"Do you?"

He opens his mouth, but quickly shuts it, as if reconsidering.

Tilting my head, I inhale deeply as his hand drifts down to my neck. Thumb stroking over my thrumming pulse.

I watch as Will pokes his tongue out to dampen his lips. The way his throat bobs with a swallow, just before his chest rises, shoulders broadening, as if bracing himself.

For someone so brash at times, he's also so very gentle.

"I do," he says simply, yet the gravity of his words tugs on my heart. "I do get it, because I know you, and I know how protective you are of what's yours." My eyes burn, and I see that burn reflected in his glistening eyes as he goes on, "I've known that since the day I met you, when you tried like hell to scare me off. When you made it clear I wasn't welcome to sit with you and your friends."

I feel my neck heat and I shake my head. "I—"

He chuckles. "It was cute."

Rolling my eyes, I turn away from his hand. He only laughs harder.

"He never did like sharing."

Whipping my head over to Mason, I glare at him as he joins us.

He shrugs, lips screwed up in a rueful smile. "Sorry. Didn't mean to eavesdrop." Taking a seat on the black leather armchair next to us, he stretches out his legs, and folds his hands loosely together over his lap. Glancing at Will he says, "It took him over a month to warm up to me when I moved to town."

Scoffing, I say, "That's a lie."

"You glared at me every time I so much as breathed in the same space as Izzy," he says chuckling, light blue eyes swimming with mirth at the memories. "Face it, man. You're kind of territorial."

I open my mouth to refute that, but Will interrupts before I can.

"Wait, you didn't always live in Shiloh?"

Frowning, I glance my boyfriend. "You didn't know that?"

His eyes are wide as he shakes his head. "No."

Huh.

"I moved to Shiloh when I was six, not long after my dad left," Mason explains. "Just from a couple towns over, so it's not like I was totally new to the area."

Shawn joins us then, gesturing for Mason to scoot a bit so he can sit on the arm.

"We good?" Mason asks.

Shawn nods. "Said they should have enough to start layering. We're free 'til tomorrow morning."

"Sweet."

Will's fingers play absently with the collar of my shirt as Mason and Shawn start discussing how we should celebrate finishing the new song. I don't even think he realizes he's doing it. His gaze is far-off, almost wistful.

"Hey."

He blinks and looks up at me. "Hey yourself."

The guys are still talking amongst themselves, and Paul and Bryce are busy over by the sound deck, their backs to us. Taking the brief moment of privacy, I press myself closer to Will, all but sinking into him as I drop my cheek to his shoulder.

He turns, pressing a kiss to my head, before burying his nose in my hair.

God, I'm gonna miss this.

"It's okay," he says softly, ensuring his words are just for my ears. "Not wanting to share all of this with the world yet."

Pulling back, I meet his steady blue gaze, searching for any traces of doubts.

"I'm not ashamed," I tell him firmly, reaching for his hand and squeezing.

His mouth tightens faintly in the corners, but for once he doesn't look like he doesn't believe me.

"I know," he chokes out quietly. "I know that. Slow, remember? It's okay to go slow. One day at a time."

Blinking rapidly, I nod. "One day at a time."

His lips rise. "I like that you're territorial."

Huffing through my nose, I shake my head. "Fuck off."

"I told you, it's cute."

Groaning, I shove his stupid, smiling face away. "Fucking asshole," I grumble.

He's about to say something, probably something infuriating, but the guys cut in before he gets the chance, announcing we're going for celebratory tattoos.

Will's face blanches and I don't bother stifling a laugh.

The guys and I always joked that we'd get matching tattoos the day we "hit it big." I wouldn't say making a breakthrough with a song counts as hitting it big, but you know what? Fuck it.

We already *did* make it big. We're here, aren't we? We hit our first of what will probably be many challenges, and we fucking overcame it. All without caving into our addictions.

We didn't give up.

If that's not a reason to fucking celebrate, I don't know what is.

8

WAYLON MCALLISTER

FIVE DAYS.

Five perfectly imperfect days.

LA is an inherently lonely city, one fueled by impossible dreams and broken hearts.

But for five long, sunshine-filled days, I got to live what so few achieve here.

Work didn't stop for anyone, least of all me. And least of all Will, who had no choice but to either watch me work or traipse around the city by himself.

But seeing him in the sound booth as I belted out lyrics written for him into a microphone had a way of making up for all that. Even though we would've much rather have spent the little time we had together alone, and preferably naked.

But watching him smile through the glass. Watching him laugh with the guys in between take after take after take...

Feeling his hand on mine, strong and warm, yet casual, and so, so easy as we walked Sunset Boulevard on the days and evenings I got a break from the studio, looking for somewhere to eat...

That's what the real dreams are made of.

Crashing into bed together at night was just the cherry on top.

"Whatcha thinkin' about?" he asks, pulling me out of my thoughts.

I squint up at the setting sun, sitting big and orange in the sky. It's a September evening in California. Not too hot, not too cold. Perfect.

Sand cushions the back of my head from under a thin white sheet we brought from the hotel. Will's sprawled out on his stomach next to me. With nothing but the soundtrack of waves crashing into the beach, it's quiet. Peaceful.

"Just wishing we had more time," I admit softly, before rolling my head toward his.

"Me too," he says just as softly. As if neither of us dare to disturb the quiet, nearly empty beach around us.

Messy, dirty blonde hair flops over his brow. Sand clings to the wavy strands, but he doesn't seem to mind. It suits him, the salt and the sand.

This is what I'll miss most, I think, making sure I ingrain this image to memory.

The sun beating down on his face, lighting up his features orange and gold like a canyon fire.

The crash of waves reflected in his navy blue eyes.

Wavy, unkempt hair burnished gold and rough from sea salt.

This boy of mine was made for California sunsets on the beach, and yet he's the one leaving tomorrow. While I remain here.

His hand reaches out, finding mine, lacing our fingers together.

I eye our matching tattoos, loving the way they seem to interlock and merge into one from this angle.

My gaze then drifts up to the inside of my wrist, where my new ink has started to scab over. It's itchy as hell, but I'm used to it by now.

It's nothing too crazy. Just a simple heartbeat design, like what you'd see on an EKG. If you line all three of our wrists together, though—Mason's, Shawn's, and mine—it connects to form one steady heartbeat.

Cheesy? Maybe.

But I love it.

"I've been thinking about going back to school," Will announces suddenly.

My head shoots up. "Really?"

He nods, biting his lip. "Can't really putz around forever, you know. The bar's great and all, but it's—"

"Not long-term for you," I finish gently, nodding in understanding. And the income is far from stable. I search his gaze. "So are you thinking of finishing your degree, or...?"

Blowing out a breath, he looks down, dark gold lashes fanning his cheeks.

"I have more than enough credits to minor in psych," he says slowly, the words dragging out, almost like he's stalling.

Frowning, I say, "So you don't want to major in it anymore, is what you're saying."

He starts nodding, but stops.

Then, suddenly, he sits up.

He faces the water with his knees pressed to his chest, arms wrapped around his shins. He's in jeans, like me, but he's not

STILL BEATING (PAPERBACK)

wearing a shirt—his faded gray AC/DC t-shirt left discarded where he was using it as a pillow.

Slowly, I join him, watching the way the sun's orange rays war with the emotions playing out on his face. Wariness mixed with something like determination.

His tanned shoulders bunch, like he's bracing himself.

"I think..." he says slowly. "I think I want to go into social work."

Oh.

My chest rises with a deep inhale and I turn to face the water so I'm no longer staring at him. I watch the rise and fall of water as the tide pulls back, then crashes forward once more. Over and over and over again.

"The system's fucked."

"Really fucked," I whisper through numb lips. I can't be sure if the roar in my ears is coming from the ocean, or my thundering heart as what he's saying sinks in.

"But maybe... maybe it doesn't have to be. Maybe the only way of fixing it, is from the inside out," he says tightly.

Some strong, unnamed emotion has me by the throat, holding my tongue hostage.

"I couldn't save you," he whispers, his words carrying on the faint ocean breeze. "I couldn't save you, but maybe, maybe I can save some other little boy. Or girl."

In the corner of my eye, I see him shake his head.

"Doesn't matter. I just—" He gulps. "The system's fucked and it's not right."

Another blink. Then another. And I'm pretty sure salt has sprayed into my eyes, because they're burning, they're burning, they're burning so hotly.

And all I can think is, *of course.*

This is Will. *Will.*

Will No-Middle-Name Foster.

Mouthy, passionate, over-protective Will.

Of course, this is what he's meant to do with his life. Of course. It's so goddamn obvious, it's laughable.

My lips start to rise just as he blurts, "Unless you think it's stupid."

I open my mouth to say something, but he doesn't give me a chance.

He whips his head around to face me, eyes troubled. "I mean, I know it's not as easy as it sounds, and I'm just getting ahead of myself. Hell, maybe this is actually a really, really bad idea for m—"

I shut him up with a hard, fierce kiss.

He stares at me wide-eyed and frozen as I pull back, clutch his cheeks and say, "It's perfect."

"Really?" He doesn't sound convinced, but he does sound hopeful. He's been thinking about this for a while. I just know it. I kind of want to slap him for not bringing it up sooner.

I nod. "If anyone could fuck shit up, it's you."

His lips rise into a wide grin. "Pretty sure that's not—"

"Shut up," I growl, slamming my mouth back on his.

Our kiss is hot and heavy, before tapering off into something soft and teasing.

"You've been thinking about this for a while, huh?" I say when we finally part.

His fingers play with my hair, and mine play with the collar of his shirt.

Shrugging, Will says, "Pretty much ever since I found out CPS failed you not once, but twice. The fact my parents tried, the fact teachers probably knew but were too scared to report it because of your dad's position..."

A muscle thrums in his jaw and he shakes his head, looking down at some spot on my chest. "Hell, maybe my parents weren't the only ones who called, which makes it even more fucked. It shouldn't feel hopeless. It shouldn't *be* hopeless."

Throat dry, I can only nod.

Shifting, he turns to face the ocean once more, but this time our fingers are interlocked and his head's on my shoulder. The sun is big and red-orange, lighting the sky up in swirls of pink as we watch it sink slowly into the horizon. Leaving behind an purplish haze on the sand and water as it disappears.

"Not quite a sunrise," he whispers.

"No," I say smiling into his blond hair, looking over his head into the distance. "Not quite."

And yet, I can't help but feel hopeful, even as the night creeps in on us from behind. As the hours tick by, drawing our time together to a close.

Today was a good day.

And the following morning, when we rush off to the airport, bleary-eyed from hardly any sleep, that hope lingers, fueling our steps to the moment we must part.

It's in the steadiness of my fingers as we walk hand in hand through a bustling airport to catch his flight to Chicago. It's in the jut of my chin as I wait for Will to check his luggage.

I inhale deeply, taking in all the sights and sounds converging on us.

The dread isn't as heavy as it was when he first arrived in LA, replaced instead by a bittersweet longing for more days like the last five.

Days filled with pink sunshine and salt-laced kisses; jostling elbows and gentle hair-tugs.

Nights filled with long steamy showers where I bite into Will's fist as he bites into my back.

Stolen hours spent touching and whispering under cool, crisp sheets that smell of the ocean, making promises only we have the key to unlock.

We're stronger this time around, I remind myself. We know what to expect. Know what the other needs, even if we can't always voice it.

He made me promise to still call him if I have another panic attack.

And I made him promise to call me when the loneliness back home becomes too much for him to bear. When his fears become louder than reason.

We'll be each other's burdens. We'll be each other's strengths. Pillars to rest upon until we can be in each other's arms once more and remember what it's like to sit under a hot pink California sunset, watching the waves crash along the beach.

Only fourteen days to go.

Eventually, we won't have to count the days anymore.

Once his bag's handed off, he turns to me with a small, knowing grin.

I suck in my cheek and shrug. *This is it.*

He takes a step forward, then another, before pausing just in front of me.

I know we're out of time, so I soak the goddamn marrow out of this moment. Hoping this right here and the five days that brought us closer together will be enough to hold me over, hold *him* over, until he flies back out two weeks from now.

Two weeks.

It's nothin' right?

His mouth crooks up into a stupid grin, blue eyes glistening like little pools. There's a question in their depths, one I'm well familiar with by now. One he shouldn't even have to ask anymore.

Especially here. In an airport, thousands of miles away from the fishbowl that is Shiloh, Pennsylvania.

I'm free here in a way I'm not back home, despite most of the town already knowing. Free to be me, the real me I'm only beginning to unearth. Free to be the guy so hopelessly in love with another guy without fear of jeers or repercussion.

It's easier, I guess, when no one knows who I am. I can almost pretend I'm someone else as I reach for Will and press my body to his, burying my face in his neck.

But I don't want to be anyone else, I decide as his arms come around me, holding me tight.

His voice is in my ear, and it's all, "Way, Way, Way."

No. I don't want to be anyone else but me. But *his.*

Even when we're apart, I'll always be his.

He steps away, brushing his lips over mine with a quiet, "See ya in two weeks, Rockstar."

"Later, City Boy."

Then he's gone, turning his back on me, and walking through the metal detectors. He grabs his carry-on, looks over his shoulder and gives me a two finger salute, before disappearing around the corner, out of sight.

I press a hand to my chest.

Still beating.

Still his.

9

WILL FOSTER

TWO MONTHS LATER

IT'S LATE, JUST AFTER midnight, when Ivy grabs my arm, hauling me out of my seat.

"They landed!" she says in a breathy rush.

Phoebe's practically bouncing on her toes, fingers pressed together in front of her lips. Her hair's thrown up into a messy top-knot that teeters to the side with her movements.

They might be even more excited than me, seeing as it's been two and a half months since they saw the guys. *But only just,* I think dryly, picturing the guy *I* haven't seen in three long weeks.

Not long, in the grand scheme of things. Not long compared to the others.

But in the grand scheme of what matters to me...

It's been three weeks too long since I left my other half in the City of Angels. An unanticipated three extra weeks, seeing as they were only supposed to be out there for eight weeks. Two months, give or take.

But they needed more time to fine-tune the album. It sucked, but it was unavoidable.

And it could've been much longer.

Fortunately, after that first hiccup, it was mostly smooth-sailing. Not just recording the album, but managing a long-distance relationship.

Not that we spent more than a few weeks apart...

Still, if someone asked us months ago if we'd be able to make it even just a *night* away from each other, let alone three weeks—our new record—without losing our fucking shit, it would've been a hell. Fucking. No.

It hasn't always been easy, but we made it work. We had to. There was no other choice. No rational one, at least, and we're far from the irrational guys we once were.

Mostly.

"There they are!" Phoebe all but squeals.

The Scranton airport is quiet—a stark contrast to LAX, or even Philly or Chicago—so her voice carries, momentarily drowning out the distant chatter and the soft rock music playing through the speakers.

This time, the final time, the guys sacrificed a direct flight in order to not have to make a long drive back to Shiloh after a day of traveling. They haven't seen their beds in over two months now, and I know they're impatient to just finally be home. Back with family. Back with all the supports they've built over the years to keep them from slipping off the edge.

They did it though. They made it on their own. Stuck together like glue and powered through until they reached the other side.

This side.

Our side.

Mason comes into view first, light blue eyes tired but lit up as he takes in Phoebe running toward him. Shawn's just behind him, and if I'm not mistaken his dark eyes light up too as she wraps her brother in a hug, and reaches an arm over her shoulder, hand outstretched, fingers wiggling.

Much to my surprise, Shawn actually meets her offered hand. It's just a quick squeeze of her fingers, but it's something. I can't see her face, but I can picture the huge, face-splitting grin as clear as if it were right in front of me.

Behind them, Waylon appears, dragging along a black suit-case, a black guitar case peeking out from over his shoulder. His mouth is twisted to the side as he watches his family reunite, before his gaze drifts beyond them to the girl standing next to me.

His gaze flickers to me as he hurriedly crosses the distance, meeting his cousin in the middle when she can no longer contain herself. They collide in a tangle of limbs as he scoops her up off the ground, swinging her around.

"Hey, Satan," I hear him say quietly.

She flicks him in the forehead and he grins widely, dimples sinking deeply in his cheeks.

She wiggles in his arms, forcing him to lower her back down.

Brushing off her jeans, she flips her black hair over her shoulder and steps back. They exchange a few quiet words I can't make out from here, before he gives her the suitcase.

Dark eyes find mine, and then he's moving toward me.

Or maybe I'm moving toward him.

I'm not sure. All I know is the distance is shrinking, finally shrinking. His face is in my hands, and my lips are being crushed under the desperate weight of his kiss.

I stumble back, so I just figure, *fuck it,* and grab him, hold-ing him for leverage. He's finally in my arms again, and I'm holding him so tight I lift him off the ground. Guitar and all.

He's grumbling into my mouth, digging his nails into my shoulders. But I don't care, I don't fucking care. We could go tumbling to the ground, for all I care.

Something tells me he doesn't mind either, if the pierced tongue flicking the back of my teeth is anything to go by.

"Asshole," he mutters against my mouth.

There's my Grumpy Bear, I think, smiling against his pouty lips.

When I lower him to his feet, I pull my head back just enough to brush the tip of my nose over his. "Hi."

"Hi back," he says, voice slightly choked. Features visibly tense. If I didn't know better, I'd think he was nervous or paranoid or ashamed.

But I do know better now.

I know he's trying not to crumble.

We're nose to nose, chest to chest. Just breathing each other in like it's been years rather than just weeks.

His hazel eyes glimmer the longer we stare at each other. I'm sure mine are just as bright.

"We did it," he whispers after a moment.

I nod against him, sobering. "We did it."

He gulps, and I squeeze my eyes shut, tightening my hold on him.

And he did it without even a single drop of alcohol, I think. Hit that one year mark and kept going, in spite of every challenge he faced.

Pride doesn't even begin to cover what I feel.

No, this won't be the last time his career takes him from me, nor will it be the last time we're tested. There's already talks of a tour to promote their new album coming out early next year. Life is just kicking off for him.

For both of us, really.

I'll be starting classes in January to get my degree in social work, which means being his own personal groupie on tour won't be possible. Not anytime soon. Not full-time at least.

But he begged me not to hold back anymore. Not with him, not with my life.

"We grow together," he said firmly. *"Together or not at all. That's the only way this works."*

Knowing his words to be true, I promised him I'd try. If he can be strong without me, I can be strong without him. And that starts with finishing what I set out to do years ago. Sure, my goals shifted a bit, but I'm here now. Here and certain I know where I want to go with this one and only life of mine.

And who I want to spend it with.

Not that I wasn't already certain of that months ago.

So if that means doing *this* all over again. Trading airport hellos for airport goodbyes... East Coast sunrises for West Coast sunsets...

Over and over and over again...

Just so one day, we could meet back here, in the middle, and stay here. Happy, fulfilled, and stronger than fucking ever, then so be it.

Bring it the fuck on. We're ready for it.

He hums against my lips. "Missed you."

My fingers stroke over his dimples. "Missed you more."

"Not possible."

Pulling back, his mouth crooks up into that wicked, bad-boy grin of his. The one that never fails to crack my chest wide open, filling it with so much love and want, it's a wonder I don't burst from it.

"Take me home, City Boy?" is all he says, voice deep and rumbly.

A deep-chested groan vibrates through my chest. "Don't have to ask me twice."

And with that, hand in hand with our family trailing us, we walk out of the airport.

Free, and together again at long last.

AFTERWORD

Thank you for picking up this book. For loving these boys so hard you wanted more. I hope you enjoyed this little glimpse into their lives as they continue working toward their hard-earned HEA.

Mason and Jeremy's book is next. *Every Breath After* will be releasing in 2023. More details to come.

⸕

Before we return to Shiloh, though, I invite you somewhere a little darker, and a lot less forgiving...

I'M THE ONE THEY'VE BEEN WAITING FOR...

little bird lost

JESSIE WALKER

This is a full-length, **dark** romantic thriller/horror novel set to release in U.S. Winter/Spring 2023. It is loosely based on the Golden Bird/Firebird mythology. It is NOT fantasy or a literal retelling. Reader discretion is advised.

Flip the page for an exclusive sneak-peek!

prelude

THIS ISN'T HOW I thought it would end.

The blood on my fingers looks black, like I've dipped them in ink. Try as I might to wash it off in the snow, the evidence of what I've done is here to stay. It's a part of who I am now, woven into the tight-knit fibers of my skin, sinking down into the marrow of my bones.

A plague of the soul, he would call this.

"Is there a cure?" I imagine myself asking him.

For a moment, I'm back in his parlor. It's just me and him, his black leather gloves, that stupid cane with its gaudy, gold falcon-head handle, and the string music playing softly from the phonograph in the corner. The fireplace is dark and vacant, as always, but it's not cold.

And for once, I'm not afraid.

He gives me a smile, one as bloody as the last one he gave me. *"Mors mihi lucrum,"* he says. But it's not his voice I hear, it's mine, cracked and brittle.

The parlor fades away, taking the music with it.

Mors mihi lucrum.

Death is my reward.

I tip my head back and stare up at the moonless sky bearing down on me.

Big fat flakes of snow hit my face, intermingling with the blood and ash streaked across my cheeks and temple.

It's cold now. So very, very cold. But I'm no longer shivering.

Somewhere in this deep, dark, wintry wood, a fire still rages on, blazing up into an indifferent night sky as it battles against the frigid temperatures. A scream into an endless, timeless void.

If a castle burns in the woods with no ears to hear, no eyes to see... I sing-song silently, a sluggish grin pulling at my frozen face.

I lift a heavy hand, reaching for the sky.

"Is it even really burning?" I finish out loud, my voice nothing more than vapor on the wind.

My bare, bloody fingers grip at nothing before they fall once more to my side.

I take a step forward, then another, eyes trained on the trees reaching for me as blackness creeps in around my vision.

I don't know how long I've been walking. How I'm even still capable of standing, let alone moving. It feels like I've been walking forever. Trudging through an endless forest on the cusp of freezing, lungs charred from smoke, fingers and soul forever stained with the blood of my crimes.

"Do you really think the world out there will be enough for you after this?" I hear him now, his voice a hiss in my head, like that of a snake twisting down from a tree limb, beckoning me. *Bite the apple. Just take one little bite.*

"Do you think they'd even want you back?"

What world? I think, head drooping as I fight to stay upright, fight to stay awake. There is no world left. There is only this. Only snow and ash and a forest that never ends.

The ground shifts, my vision tilting, trees stretching and twisting. Somewhere I think I can hear wings flapping in the wind. Chirps and calls that are weak and somber.

I stumble, blink, and I'm suddenly on my knees. Another blink, and I'm sprawled out on my side. Dark red hair fans out around my face, snow crystallizing the strands.

JESSIE WALKER

"Get up," a voice tells me. It's one and yet it's not. It's *more.* It's many. And their voices are pleading.

But the air is heavy. My limbs, even heavier. And my eyes, the heaviest of them all.

In my head, I hear familiar chanting as the darkness welcomes me. It grows louder and louder until it reaches deafening decibels. And yet, somehow, it doesn't drown out the broken voices still urging me to get up, begging me to keep going.

I can't, I try to tell them, fingers flexing toward that pitch-black sky. *I'm sorry.*

For a moment, it all stops. The chanting, the pleas, the flapping of wings.

Everything just... stills. And that's when I hear *him.* Clear as day, exactly as I remember, for the first time in... I don't know how long. Years, I imagine.

"Can you see the moon? It's huge here."

My breath hitches, and this time, I don't take another one.

No, I respond to him silently as understanding finally sinks in. *No, I don't see it.*

The moon is hidden from me. It's always... been... hidden...

"Do you see now?" the snake hisses as my thoughts slow. *"Do you finally get it, dear?"*

Somewhere in the distance, a crow caws mournfully into the night, and all I can think is, *I tried. I tried so hard...*

If I could still cry, I'd never stop.

If my heart could still break, it'd shatter completely.

But I can't, it can't. I'm fading, I'm losing, I'm already gone.

Because the moon doesn't shine on dead girls.

And I've been marked for death a long, long time.

*this excerpt is unedited and subject to change

Sign up for Jessie Walker's **newsletter** for updates on future projects, early sneak-peaks, and bonus material.

www.authorjessiewalker.com

⚹

Join Jessie Walker's official reader group **The Black Sheep** on Facebook.

ACKNOWLEDGEMENTS

Every single person who put up with me these last few weeks...

Thank you.

This release happened in a whirlwind, and there are so many people who helped me not only get this novella in tip-top shape, but worked with very little notice to help me get everything in place.

Heather, my editor. We couldn't have planned the timing better if we tried. Thank you for working so tirelessly and diligently, hashing out any issues we ran into, and encouraging me throughout. It's always a comfort to know my babies are in good hands.

Gloria, my alpha and sanity. You saw me at my most neurotic with this one. Thank for for the endless chats, for reassuring me when I just wanted to scrap it all and run away. I'm always throwing books at you, making you cry, and blowing up your inbox with all my worries over every little thing... and yet, somehow, you still put up with me.

Tasha and Nat, my beta readers. Thank you for taking the time to read my surprise little book in such short-notice. Your feedback helped me tremendously with filling in any gaps, and helping me ensure this story stayed true to itself.

Chelsea and Dee, my very own PA Dream Team. You guys came in right when I needed you most. I look forward to seeing where this journey takes us.

My Wailers! — Thank you for all the help promoting this novella. I'm so excited to finally have a Street Team of my very own. I can't wait to spoil you rotten.

All other bloggers and instagrammers who helped me get the word out, shared teasers, promoted this book... I couldn't have managed such a surprise, last-minute release without you.

Lastly, the ones who made this novella possible in the first place. The ones who still always want "more" despite having had 300k+ words already. The ones who continue to share their love for these boys and my words, and find comfort in this world. Y'all are greedy and I adore you endlessly. I can't wait to take us back to Shiloh.

CONTENT WARNING

Triggers: addiction, mental illness (panic attacks/PTSD), grief, past mentions of abuse, past mentions of suicidal thoughts/ideations

ABOUT THE AUTHOR

Jessie Walker is a New Adult/Contemporary romance author based out of Scranton, Pennsylvania, where she lives with her long-time partner and fur-spawn. Drawn to all things dark and twisted, nitty and gritty, she likes to pretend she's not the hopeless romantic at heart that she is. When she's not drudging away at a keyboard, there's a very good chance you'll find her vegged out on her couch, listening to sad '90s grunge, and dreamin' up all the ways she can make the voices in her head suffer (just so she could put them back together again). She has a BS in Psychology, and will diagnose you.

Goodreads | Amazon | Website

Instagram | Facebook

Made in United States
Troutdale, OR
09/15/2023

12919988R00102